This book is dedicated to my dog Buddy,
who was the definition of a fighter.

"Got room for one more?"

—Major Marquis Warren

CONTENTS

P.S. CHECK OUT THE PRINCE'S JOURNAL FOR A PLACE TO WRITE YOUR OWN NOTES ABOUT THE STORY AND ITS SUSPECTS

FOREWORD

The year was 2021. In the midst of trying to get a mechanical engineering degree, barely a sophomore at the time, Chad Nicholas was enrolled in a single theater class, one of the university's core classes. A welcomed break from the seemingly endless math of his major, the class was focused on the history of filmmaking and appreciation of those who made it possible.

The class project? Write a ten-page screenplay based on the Brothers Grimm fairy tales.

Naturally, Chad decided to have fun with it.

Rather than a straight adaption, he wanted to create something new.

Before long, the story began to take form. Soon the ten pages became fifteen, then twenty, then thirty, until finally, one hundred and thirty-four pages later, the screenplay was finished. Luckily, the professor forgave the "slight" breaking of the page count and actually gave a few points of extra credit. With that, the course was over.

But Chad couldn't stop thinking about the story.

What started as a fun, lighthearted project had become a story that he truly cared about, and so, after having finished the first draft of *The Animal* just a few months prior, he decided to adapt the screenplay into what would become his fourth novel.

A few years later, a lot has changed. Chad's graduated college, *The Animal*'s been released.

And the new fairy tale is finally ready.

Countless hours were spent writing the story in between classes, countless more spent editing it, both by him and his incredible editor, Eliza Dee, not to mention various proofreads, and the amazing work of Miblart, who designed the cover, the interior artwork, and the formatting.

All that work was done with one goal in mind: Give the readers something special.

With all that said, Chad is incredibly grateful that you chose this book.

More than anything, he hopes it will make you smile.

And maybe scream… just a little.

Welcome to *One Grimm Night*.

ONE GRIMM NIGHT

PART ONE:
THE GIRL IN RED

CHAPTER ONE

You've heard the legends…

Complete darkness shrouds the land: a darkness so strong, so violent, that the mere memory of light, of color, is but a distant shadow, blotted out and cast away like a long-forgotten relic of a past life, replaced only by the blackness, the emptiness of shadows and decay. The dwelling place of dark things. Evil things.

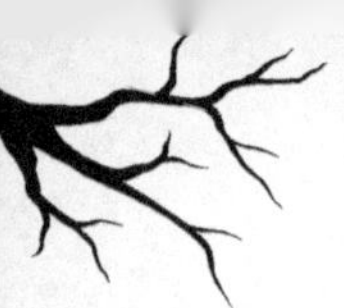

The stories told of monsters haunting these woods…

Within the vast grip of nothingness lies the forest, endless trees stretching out over the dying land, filling it with hollow trunks and rotting bark that falls like black, decaying snow. Yet worst of all are the branches: horrific, twisting high, splintering themselves apart as they distort further with each passing day, some spiraling into their own destruction, others breaking apart from themselves fully, cracking wood moaning with agony into the night.

Of the creatures born in the darkness that hunt those born in the light…

Thunder howls in the sky as lightning crawls down from above, scorching the night's air in brightness for only a moment as rain pours from the formless grey clouds looming overhead, drenching the land in a downpour so thick and consuming that the forest can barely be seen through it: thousands of piercing droplets falling down so violently that it is as if the storm were trying to drown the very forest itself.

You've heard the screams, the cries of the victims consumed by the darkness within.

The ones who couldn't escape the horrors…

Caught within the storm, within the cloudburst of elements and the forest of fallen twilight that lies beneath it, illuminated by the violent flash of lightning, is the girl in red.

Streaks of crimson flash in the night as she runs, tripping in the mud that surrounds her. The soft, scattered

soil tries to drag her down into its suffocating depths as she passes through the endless expanse of everblack oaks, whose broken branches almost seem to be reaching out to her, attempting to choke her within their grasp.

Yet the forest is not what she fears.

No, she is afraid of something far darker: the nightmarish thing that lurks within, the thing that even the darkness is afraid of.

The tales are true. Every last legend.

Every scream, every horror, every tragic detail.

Save for one…

For a lifetime the girl runs, even as the rain falls upon her and the forest grows around her, through woods that seem to have no end, the red of her hood the only color that appears in its dark expanse. A single color within a night of pitch black and precious little white. Yet still she runs until she feels as though her feet would collapse, her lungs would tire and her body would force her to the dirt, all the while her heart still cries out, wishing for escape from this living grave into which she has so foolishly fallen.

All she wanted was to escape. Escape the pain.

Not knowing that it is pain upon which this forsaken forest feeds.

Eventually, even the crimson streaks of her hood are once again choked out by the woodland shadows, and the black nothingness returns, shrouding her cries, keeping the

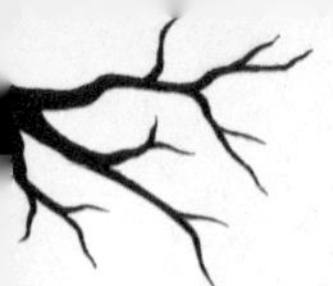

life hidden in the gloom, where it might as well not have existed. Such is the story of her life: cries of anguish unheard, pleas for help unnoticed, nightmares uncomforted, until at last she wondered why she bothered screaming at all.

Here in this forest, the hopelessness has found her again.

Finally, she collapses, crying out one last time in agony, not from injury, or in seeking help, but from the final acceptance of death.

Whatever comes, it could never be as cruel as life.

A life with no light. No life at all.

Darkness eternal.

Yet as her cries echo through every corner of the twisted thicket, her pain felt by everything that breathes within it, suddenly a single light appears, flickering in the distance. A single ember, all alone against the black grip of death. Signaling life. Signaling hope.

The legends say the horrors were decades apart…

Desperation growing with each passing moment, bones rattling in sheer terror of what might lurk in the nothingness behind her, the girl in red runs towards the light.

That the stories never connected…

In the midst of the dark forest, as thunder shakes the very ground and frenzied strikes of lightning twist unnaturally around the rainfall, the crimson hood grows

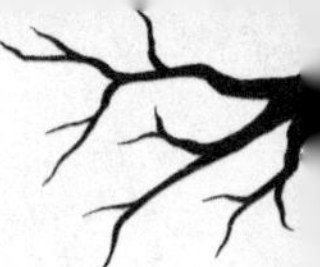

closer to the light, until finally the girl in red can see its source reflecting in her eyes, see her only hope for escaping the distorted nightmare trapping her.

In the darkness, she sees the cabin.

But that's a lie. A twisted fantasy, too sweet to be reality…

The cabin stands within the wicked woodland, its decaying oak creaking against the force of the storm, yet it does not fall. It holds its ground in the gloom, and from within its old walls and cracked windows, a light flickers. Beyond it, in the shadow of the forest, a desperate hand covered in dirt beats against the door.

In truth…

Cries for help echo from the girl shrouded in a hood of red.

It all happened on a single night…

CHAPTER TWO

Crimson hood glowing in the moonlight, Red cries out into the night as she beats desperately against the cabin's door, begging for an escape from the forest's cold grasp, the terror of what she has seen lurking within still echoing in the depths of her tear-filled eyes. Echoes of fangs, fur and, most of all, fright.

"Help me!"

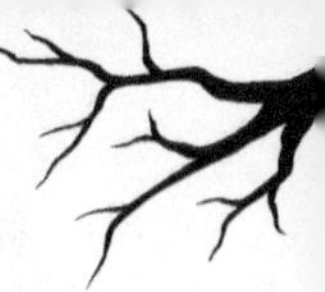

The cabin door does not open, nor does any response come from inside its walls, and a shudder of unimaginable dread creeps down Red's shivering spine. She longs for the safety within—so close, yet locked away from her reach—and fears dying here, so close to salvation. Even now she can feel the monster's breath on her neck.

Red beats against the door again, her cracked voice growing more desperate with each cry.

"Please, help me!"

Receiving no sign of life from within the cabin's locked walls, Red slowly turns to the forest once more, not willing to go back into its depths, not willing to become trapped in the shadows now swirling in the storm as if circling the moon itself. A tear falls from her cheek as she hits the door with her dirt-covered hand one last time, the desperate plea of a girl already in death's shade.

"Please," she weeps. "Help me."

The door opens.

Falling to the floor of the cabin, a terrified soul not feeling the pain of impact, Red crawls desperately across the wooden floor, not waiting for an invitation nor caring what awaits inside, only seeking to get further from the door, from the sight of the forest, lest the darkness lurking outside reach in and drag her back out.

A trail of shimmering blood is left behind her as she crawls, originating from a large gash carved into her leg, remnants of the horror forever scarred upon her body. It is one of many scars that litter her pale skin, but at the moment it is the only one she can remember, the only one given to her not by mortal cruelty but by some nightmare she couldn't fathom.

By the door, an old woman stands perfectly still, watching Red with a tilted head. Her face is full of concern, echoed within her soft words.

"What's wrong, dear?"

Backed into the creaking wall of the cabin, wishing she could shrink within it, Red stares across the small space, over the bloodied trail she's left behind and straight through the open door at the forest looming outside. As she speaks, fear chokes the words in her throat, causing them to come out hoarse and broken.

Yet through the pain, she makes a single request.

"Close it."

Hearing the girl's words, and yet not heeding their importance, the old woman notices the blood. "Good heavens," she says, "you're bleeding."

Red's gaze doesn't leave the door, or that which lies behind it, as the horrific things she's witnessed flash before her eyes like sparks of a fire. Through tears, she begs once more.

"Close it!"

With a sympathetic nod, the old woman at last closes the door, keeping the rain from creeping inside, blocking the lightning and muffling the thunder. Hiding the forest from view, as though the cabin were now all that existed.

The moment the sight of it is cut off from her vision, Red feels salvation cascade over her as if she had escaped the clutches of death itself, and crying tears of unknown relief, perhaps the first time she's ever felt it, she looks to the old woman with eyes of gratitude. "Thank you."

Without a second's hesitation, the old woman hurries over to her, the girl still huddled up on the floor, soaked in rain and shivering uncontrollably, remnants of the danger outside still lingering on her skin even in safety.

"You must be freezing, child."

Gently, so as not to spook the trembling girl, the old woman kneels down and looks into her terrified eyes with sympathy, removing the large wool scarf from her own neck and gently placing it around Red's shoulders, drying the rain and providing a moment's warmth.

The fireplace burns bright beside them, sparks of embers floating gently in the air before turning to ash and vanishing from sight as quickly as they came, and within this momentary phenomenon, the old woman smiles at the girl, but Red doesn't yet return her gaze. As the ash withers away before their eyes, the old woman looks down, once again noticing the gash carved into Red's leg.

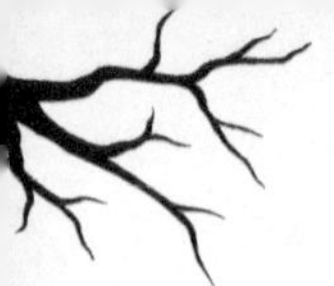

"We need to get that cleaned and wrapped up."

The old woman reaches out, attempting to take the girl's hand, to lead her to the chair where the wound might be cleaned, but Red jumps at her touch, eyes still unwilling to leave the door for fear the horror might return the moment she lets it fall from her sight.

"You don't have to be afraid, child." Offering Red a motherly smile, the old woman touches her cheek, wiping away a trembling tear, breaking her free from her trance of terror. "You are safe now."

Red's frightful gaze finally leaves the door.

At last, she looks to the old woman, nodding softly, her eyes filled with overwhelming gratitude, and another tear.

"Thank you."

Blood drips softly from the exposed wound, falling slowly through the air and staining the wooden floor beneath as crimson as the hood the girl still wears. Eventually, it seeps through even the cracks within the floor, falling still further down into the earth, until finally the old woman takes a washcloth, dripping wet itself, and cleans the wound.

The wound is deep: one large gash along the length of Red's calf. While not fatal, it left behind a trail of blood on the floor as a testament to the pain it has caused, and the scar that will be left as a reminder of what she has suffered,

the monster to which she has borne witness. Still, even as the old woman presses against the wound, Red doesn't move or even wince; instead, she only looks out through the nearest window, searching through the pouring rain for eyes of scarlet, listening for heavy footsteps hidden within the booming thunder. As lightning cracks in the sky, its light reaching in and bathing her face in flashes of pure white, she pulls her red hood closer to her face, almost trying to hide within it.

It does not escape the old woman's notice.

"What is it that has you so frightened, child?"

Hands trembling, lips quivering, Red tries to answer. "It's…"

Memories once evanesced flood into her mind in an instant, visions of rotting oak and bark-covered shadows as she runs between them.

"There's something in the forest."

The forest seemed endless. It was endless. As though it were growing around her. As though she were growing around it.

Becoming part of its feast.

"It chased me."

Limping, she stumbled within the woods, crying out for help as a massive shadow loomed behind her. A shadow darker than the forest itself.

"The sound it made as it hunted me…" Her skin goes pale and her eyes glassy as she stares into nothing, reliving the moment, feeling as though the mere memory might stop her heart from beating. "I thought… I thought I was going to die."

The old woman offers another kind smile and softly pats the girl's shoulders, bringing her back from the trenches of her nightmarish memories and once more into the light of reality, where the fire burns bright beside them. "Come now, dear, you're safe now. The forest might be dangerous, but my home is not."

A moment later, no more blood falls from the wound, and the old woman finishes cleaning it before gently wrapping an old scarf around the girl's torn calf, careful not to hurt her. Finally, she cautiously reaches up, talking hold of the red hood that rests over the girl. At first Red's hands raise up to meet hers, hesitancy at another's touch, at her covering being removed, but when she sees the old woman's smile, her anxiety is soothed and she relents, allowing the old woman to slowly lower the hood, revealing Red's face to her for the first time.

"My goodness," she says, looking at Red in amazement, her fair skin, her bright green eyes, and most of all her glowing red hair that shimmers in the light of the fire. "What's a pretty young thing like you doing out here in these woods all by yourself?"

Red looks down to the floor, her eyes betraying her hesitation. "I was looking for my family. They live on the other side of the forest."

A solemn sigh of sorrow slips from the old woman's voice. "I know what it is like to come somewhere expecting to find family, only to find heartache." She smiles. "But it's okay. You'll see your family in no time. For now, we'd best keep you out of the storm. Its dreadful tonight."

Standing up, the old woman helps Red do the same and slowly leads her through the dimly lit cabin, past the fire and to a bedroom in the farthest corner within the wooden walls. Once inside, she motions to a small cot, upon which lie several blankets, only a few, but more than Red has been given in all her life.

"You can rest here. The storm doesn't look like it will let up anytime soon, and we are still a few hours from daylight in any case. Once morning comes, you are free to stay here as long as you wish."

Red sees the cot, the blankets to keep her warm from the rain still drenching her hair and dripping down to her shoulders; she hears the promise of safety from the violence still echoing within the forest. Is this the comfort most know all their lives? That which she dared enter this forest to find? Another tear almost escapes the green of her eyes as she hugs the old woman tight.

"Thank you."

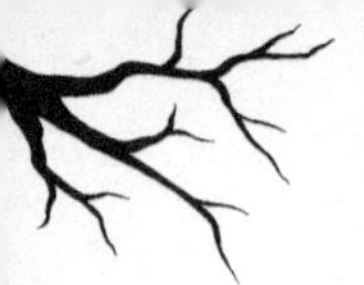

"You're very welcome."

Moonlight glows brightly in the window, violent rain caught in the wind's grasp crashes down upon the roof above, and thunder shakes the entire cabin, so loud that it echoes in her bones.

Closing her eyes and attempting to block out the noise, to remove herself from the storm's reach, Red whispers quietly to herself. "You're safe now."

She breathes deep, holding her red hood close as if it might protect her, keep her safe from the horrors of this world.

"You're safe."

A few seconds of calm pass, until she almost believes it: that she is safe not only from the storm, from the shadows of the trees, but from what lies beyond it. Safe from what she entered the forest to escape.

The scars gained while she hid in her hood.

But then, striking through the momentary calm, a muffled sound echoes from below, causing her eyes to open wide, flashes of lightning reflecting in them as she listens.

It begins muffled, but soon the creaking of wood grows louder, more insidious with each passing second until it can no longer be ignored, forcing her to lean over the edge of the cot, waiting for another sound.

At first, nothing comes.

But then the creaking returns once again, more violent than before, growing louder and more twisted with each moment it echoes, like the depths of the cabin that her blood had sunk to were crying out, begging for protection against being swallowed up by the raging storm.

The horrific noise steals the light from Red's eyes as she grows afraid once more.

Then, something changes.

All at once, a loud *crash!* echoes from below.

The sound shakes Red's bones as she jumps back in shock.

Then, absolute silence.

For the rest of the night, Red lies shaking on the small cot, hiding within her hood, waiting for another terrifying sound that never comes.

Outside, the light from the cabin's fire disappears in the night, and the cabin is once more trapped in the darkness of the forest and the storm that has consumed it.

CHAPTER THREE

In the morning light of the rising sun, Red wakes up, opening her sleepy eyes to see an old man standing only a few feet away from the cot where she rests. At first she thinks it a nightmare, a memory of visits in the

night, but it is no illusion. There he stands, staring right at her, as if he had been watching her sleep.

She recoils in shock at the sight of him. Old, leathery skin, wrinkled brow, coarse strands of hair so grey they almost appear white, and while he appears small in stature, this is due not to physical limitations but rather the nature of his hunched-over posture and dark demeanor. Long, bony arms hang close to his sides, and his head protrudes sharply from his bent-over neck, yet his weary eyes remain focused on her as she stares back in confused disbelief.

Paying no mind to her shocked expression, the old man grunts.

"The girl's up," he snarls. Then he simply leaves, not having spoken a word to Red, only cutting his eyes towards her as if her presence somehow offended him.

Left alone, Red stays in bed a moment longer, calming her spooked heart and looking out through the window at the forest looming outside. The rising sun might have illuminated its features and cast out the darkness, but the storm remains, seeming to have grown more violent in the light of day. Wind shakes the trees and tears their branches asunder, whistling a tune of destruction. Rain falls from the sky as though the day itself were crying out in sorrow at the cursed night to come.

Alone in the small room, Red shudders and holds her crimson hood close.

Limping slightly on her wounded leg, trying to hide the pain coursing from it, Red moves through the cabin, seeing its features clearly for the first time. Wood lines its walls, not allowing even a drop of rain to reach within. Furniture decorates the floors, old chairs long faded yet still sturdy beyond their years.

On the far side stands the black chimney of a fireplace, the remnants of a flame still lingering within, glowing orange embers and ash floating in the air trapped inside the rusted metal frame.

Beyond the fireplace, Red finds the kitchen, where the old woman who saved her life now stands, cheerfully making tea.

"Good morning, child!"

Red smiles, but her voice comes out quiet. "Good morning."

"I hope my friend didn't startle you. I asked him to see if you were awake."

"Oh," Red says, shaking her head. "No, he didn't."

The old woman chuckles. "You are too kind to lie, aren't you? It's okay, he startles most people."

Looking across the cabin, Red's gaze once again finds the old man, sitting in a worn-down chair and staring intently into nothing. "Is he your…"

"Husband?" The old woman smiles, thinking it funny. "Oh, goodness no. Just an old friend who came to visit. The storm trapped him here same as it did you. I would have introduced you last night, but he gets a bit grumpy if he's woken up."

Red nods. "That's all right."

"So," the old woman asks, pouring tea from its pot, beautiful steam rising from the porcelain like ghosts escaping their graves, "how did you sleep?"

"Good," Red says at first, even as the haunting sound of creaking wood echoes in her mind. "I…"

She stops, not sure if she should say it.

Noticing her pause, the old woman offers a concerned smile. "What is it, dear?"

Red responds with the truth, a faint hint of dread in her voice. "I heard something last night."

"Wood cracking?"

Red nods.

The old woman winks.

"I heard it too. It's this old place." She gestures around the cabin, at its walls of wood, its roof of oak. "It's too old. Like me. Its bones are not as strong as they once were. It can still weather the storm, but not without a little creaking now and then."

Relief does not yet wash over Red, as the other haunting sounds remain in her memory. "I also heard a crash from beneath me. As if it were coming from the ground."

The old woman nods. "The basement. I went down last night to get some wood for the fire and accidentally knocked over a lantern. Lucky I didn't catch the house on fire with my carelessness. But I'm sorry if I woke you."

"No, that's okay," Red says as the rhythm of her heart becomes peaceful once more. "I was just curious is all."

The old woman smiles and offers her tea, but Red shakes her head.

"I don't want to impose. It's light out now. I should be able to make it to my family's house before nightfall."

"Nonsense. You are not imposing, and I wouldn't feel right sending you out there in the middle of this storm. You'd no doubt get lost in the forest."

They look through the paned glass window in the kitchen's center, barely able to see the trees through the rain. In the distance, thunder echoes.

"Are you sure?" Red asks. "You've already…"

"Of course," the old woman replies without a second's hesitation. "Besides, it's not often I get company. I haven't had a visitor in years. Aside from him, of course…" She points to the haggard old man still sitting in his chair. "But he's not one for conversation."

The old man grunts in response.

"Thank you," Red says as grateful tears begin to form in her emerald eyes.

"No need to thank me, child." She gently pats Red's shoulder, which remains covered by a hood of crimson velvet. "However, if you might permit me a question?"

"Of course."

The old woman hands Red a cup of pink porcelain, and they take a seat around the large wooden dining table, enjoying the light of the morning and the warmth of the tea.

"Why were you traveling through the forest in the first place? With all the stories told of these woods, I would have thought you'd have taken the north road to your family's house."

"Stories?" Red inquires.

The old woman's posture changes, and her eyes reflect shock. "You haven't heard the stories told of this forest?"

"No."

Disbelief echoes in the old woman's words. "Your family sent for you without warning you about the legends? I find that hard to believe."

Red looks down, suddenly tense, hiding her eyes back within her hood.

The old woman chuckles, eyes almost accusatory. "Hard to believe indeed."

A few moments pass. Rainfall echoes beyond the cabin's walls, and the tension of the unspoken accusation

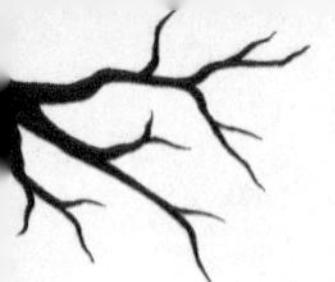

subsides. Red speaks once more, seeking an answer most wish they did not know. "What do the stories say?"

"Oh… they tell of a monster who lives in these woods. Something born of the night itself. They also whisper tales of children entering this forest, never to escape, never to be seen again."

A dark recollection flashes in Red's mind, the haunting image of a monstrous shadow chasing her only hours before. "Are the stories true? The ones about the children?"

"I don't know" is her answer. "Honestly, I find most of it to be exaggerated delusions. Some child comes in these woods, sees a shadow, and thinks a monster is after them."

The old woman pauses for a moment, staring off into the forest lurking just outside the window, forever watching them.

"But I do believe something is wrong with this forest. It twists and winds in a way that is unnatural, almost as if it were alive." Sparks of dreadful memories flash in her aged eyes. "Once, I went for a five-minute walk, and it took me four hours to find my way home. I think that is where the stories come from. From children who got lost within the trees and merely couldn't find their way back out."

The old woman gently reaches over and pats Red's hand, offering a kind smile.

"That is why I am hesitant to let you go back out there. Even on the clearest of days, this forest grows, changes. In

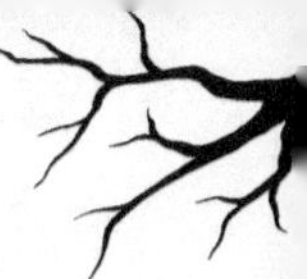

the middle of a storm, I am afraid you wouldn't be able to find your way out."

Red nods, hiding the relief still coursing through her once-trembling bones, thankful that she doesn't have to go back out there, back into the shadow's grasp. Thankful to have safety, even if only for a moment.

A place to play pretend that she is the happy child she should have been.

"What about you?" Red finally asks, genuine curiosity in her youthful voice. "If you've heard the stories, why did you come here?"

The old woman chuckles and leans back in her chair, looking off into the distance for a moment. "For the same reason as you, I suppose. For family. I had heard stories told that my sister was here, in these woods, and I came to find her."

"Did you?"

"No," the old woman sighs, sadness echoing in her words. "I searched this entire forest, and the town surrounding it. But I've never found a trace of her. It's as if she simply vanished."

A pause lingers as the old woman composes her solemn words.

"By the time I finally stopped looking, these woods had become my home. But sometimes I still look out these windows and expect to see her out there. The only family I have left, there somewhere in the trees, looking for me as well." The pain-filled words fall softly from her lips as she looks out into the forest, alive yet filled with shadows of death. "But more likely she is lost to me forever."

Red's heart breaks for the old woman, understanding all too well the misery of feeling alone. "Maybe she left this place?"

"Perhaps," the old woman says before her tone becomes suddenly sharp. "Or perhaps the villagers in the nearby town had something to do with her disappearance."

Shock takes hold of Red. "Why would you think that?"

"This town, these people. They never liked my family." As she speaks, her tone changes further, becoming sharper, almost angry, even as a trembling sorrow stains her eyes. "People can be cruel, child. Even the ones who act as if they are kind. Sometimes they are the cruelest of all."

Suddenly uncomfortable, Red shifts in her chair. In the far corner of the small cabin, the old man cuts his eyes to them, seemingly concerned about the old woman's silence. It grows for a moment longer until it fades as quickly as it began and the old woman's kind nature returns.

"Forgive me, child," she pleads, sensing Red's tension. "I didn't mean to unsettle you with old wounds of my past. I am truly sorry."

"It's all right," Red says with a genuine heart. Rain crashes down on the roof above them. "Really."

The old woman grins, nodding her thanks. "You are a very kind child, to put up with the ramblings of an old woman. Your parents must be very proud."

Red hesitates to respond.

The old woman notices.

"You haven't told me your name," Red says suddenly, hoping to change the subject.

"Oh," the old woman says in surprise. "You may call me Ruth. Come to think of it, I don't believe you have told me yours either."

"I'm Red."

"That's a pretty name," Ruth exclaims. "It's nice to meet you, Red." She looks out to the storm once more. "A blessing of good company. As it appears as though we are going to be stuck with each other for a while."

Thunder booms, shaking the cabin, even reaching inside and rattling their bones. The wind picks up, slinging rain against the house as if trying to scratch its way inside. Through the window they see the moon finally vanish completely, replaced by the risen sun, its light dulled by the gloom of grey clouds scattered ominously across the morning sky.

In the center of it all, the cabin creaks and its wood cries out, yet it does not fall, weathering the storm. The only calm haven within the violent forest.

"Better hope they don't come looking for you."

The old man's harsh words ring out within the small room, causing Red to turn in shock, finding him still sitting in his chair, staring at the wall.

"What?"

"Your family," the old man responds with an uncaring tone. "If they come looking for you in this weather, they'll be dead before nightfall. Maybe sooner."

Red opens her mouth to respond, but no sound can leave her lips as his words take hold of her thoughts and send a trembling chill down her spine.

Ruth turns to the old man in anger. "Why would you say such a thing?"

"It's true and you know it," the old man scoffs. "Ain't nothing that could survive out there."

Defiantly, Ruth points to Red. "She did."

"The girl got lucky. The brats always do. But there's no point in telling her lies about what'll happen if her family comes in here after her. They'll wind up dead, all because she didn't have the common sense not to wander into the middle of the woods."

Unable to speak, Red can only listen with reluctant ears and a brittle heart. A single stream of blood begins to run softly down her leg, a reminder of the wound inflicted upon her mere hours ago.

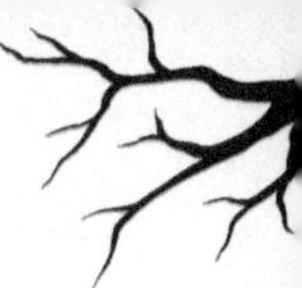

"Stop it," Ruth says, eyes flashing with concern for Red's heart as she growls at the old man to end his tales.

"Why? She might as well know now."

The old man's tone is lifeless, uncaring that Red is horrified, and as he speaks, not another sound is heard. Not the echo of rainfall, or the cries of thunder.

"The stories are true. Nothing that comes into these woods during a storm like this leaves on the other side. That's why the animals left, why the birds don't dare come here anymore. Why everything in this forsaken place is starving to death, why we're all trapped in here until we rot. Because there is nothing living, nothing natural, that could survive out there. Nothing!"

As he still speaks the words, it happens.

Suddenly, something crashes into the cabin's door, stopping their hearts from beating in an instant. From the haunting echo of the impact, it sounds as though something has almost cracked the wood and made it inside.

Red jumps back at once, all traces of calm leaving her eyes, replaced by a fear of the unknown, terror growing ever greater as she sees Ruth staring at the door in utter shock. Even the old man grows uneasy, hands nigh upon trembling as they all wait for another sound. Some sign of what's outside, what else is with them in this forest; for in their hearts they know it was more than a wayward branch adrift in the wind.

Whatever it was, it was intentional. It was living.

And it has found them.

Though no further sound comes, the echo of the first crash still haunts their thoughts, paralyzing them for a moment longer. Finally, it is Ruth who moves closer to the door, ready to discover the source of the crash, whatever else might breathe within these woods.

"Don't," Red pleads, violent memories illuminated in her eyes, proven true by the line of blood still running down her calf and creeping onto the floor beneath.

Ruth turns to her, offering a reassuring nod of safety. After a moment's hesitation, she slowly opens the cabin door, revealing what lies on the other side, the source of their awestruck fear.

Lightning flashes. Thunder echoes.

Shock takes hold, crawling over their faces as the three of them look down, seeing what has come from the forest, what has disturbed their moment of quiet safety.

A man, lying in the mud beneath them, breathing but unconscious, surrounded only by the rain and the trees, appearing as though death had taken him away long ago, leaving only his corpse behind, a reminder of the fate that befalls those trapped within this forest.

Lightning strikes once more.

PART TWO:
THE STRANGER

CHAPTER FOUR

Not a word is spoken as they stare down at the stranger, who now lies still in the mud beneath them. If not for the slight appearance of breathing, they would have thought him long dead; the outlines of his ribs are clearly revealed within his flesh, his limbs appearing as nothing more than the bones hidden inside them, merely wrapped in a layer of skin to make the skeleton appear human.

There is no motion to him at all, no sign of restless eyes or shivering skin, save for a slight shudder within his bones, as if they were attempting to crawl away while the unconscious body still held them down. The movement is small, almost imperceptible, but it is there all the same, and whether it is truly a sign of life or the nerves of a corpse still firing, they do not yet know.

"Is he dead?" Red asked, shock not leaving her face.

Ruth kneels down cautiously and places her hand on his neck, feeling for a pulse. She finds it.

"No," she answers. "But almost. We must get him inside."

She turns to the old man, expecting help. Instead, he remains still, his eyes like thick fog in the aftermath of a storm, blocking their color from view.

"Help me carry him in," she finally says, hoping to break him free from his fear induced fever.

Yet the old man still doesn't move, not acknowledging her words, not even breathing as his frightful eyes move back and forth: from the stranger on the ground to the forest from whence he undoubtedly came. Finally, his paralysis is broken, and he speaks a whisper of horror.

"Not right."

Ruth scoffs, but a dread-filled curiosity fills Red's heart as she listens to the old man's haunting words.

"Not right."

His gaze shifts to the forest once again, and the vicious storm that shakes the very trees from their roots.

"Couldn't survive. Couldn't find us."

Trembling eyes stare back at the stranger lying in the mud and the rain, as if the presence of another has sent a chill down even his old, cruel spine, causing his words to come out broken and hysterical.

"Not right. Not right. Not right."

Finally, having had enough of this madness, Ruth cuts her eyes to her old friend, barking an order. "Hush. Enough foolishness. Help me carry him in."

Still, the old man stands frozen, eyes full of suspicion as he stares down at the stranger who came to their doorstep.

"Now!" Ruth growls.

At last, fear loosens its hold over him and the old man relents. With the effort of moving a deer's corpse picked clean to the bone by wolves, they pick the stranger up from the dirt and carry his breathing corpse into their home, into their cabin.

Red stands at the edge of the door a moment longer, seeing the rain pouring from the sky and running through the dirt, feeling the shake of thunder. The storm looms overhead, trapping the poor souls caught within it.

In the distance, she sees a faint glow, the light of the morning sun trying desperately to reach the green

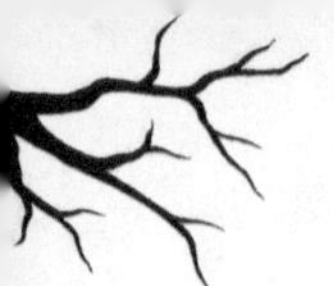

earth beneath it, choked out by grey clouds that move like formless beasts in the sky, feeding off its light and spreading their darkness.

As Red starts to move back inside, leaving the storm and the forest behind her, she notices something, a single detail that has escaped the others' perception. On the outside of the door lies a mark. A piece of wood almost caved in, its dark bark splintered, revealing the lighter brown wood within. A few distorted lines run across it, seemingly carved into it.

Red shudders and moves inside, closing the door tight behind her.

CHAPTER FIVE

"Is he breathing?" Red asks, staring down at the body. The stranger lies on the small cot, body shivering from the rain that still covers him. His sudden twitches imply a restless, perhaps painful sleep.

"Yes, child, he is breathing," Ruth answers. "But I fear he won't be for much longer."

The old man scoffs as if this were good news, taking a final frightened look at the stranger before moving away and out of sight. While he'd claim it was due to boredom, his expression betrayed his eagerness to get away from the stranger, dying or not.

But while the old man leaves, Red notices the violent shivering and only moves closer, taking off her hood and gently placing it over the man, hoping it might dry the rain, keep him warm just as it always has her.

Sadness echoes in her voice as she looks down upon the poor, dying soul. "What do you mean, not for much longer?"

"Well, given the slowness of his breathing and the way his lungs seem to choke on the air, I don't think he is in good health, even out of the storm." Ruth looks over the man, eyes glowing with curiosity. "The fact that he made it this far in the storm is quite remarkable. If indeed he wakes, I look forward to hearing how he found us."

Her eyes cut back towards Red, and a mistrustful tone echoes in her voice.

"And *why...*"

With that said, she leaves Red alone with the stranger.

Eyes filled with sympathy, Red looks down upon him, studying his features. He appears much older than her, yet nowhere near the age of Ruth or the old man, and his hair is dark, perhaps darker than the night itself.

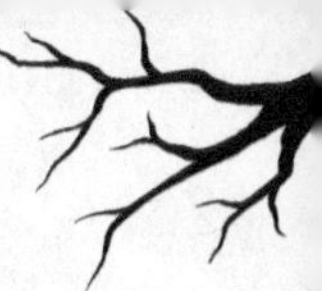

Every few seconds, the stranger's body twitches violently, as if his skeleton were trying to escape his body. As if something were hunting him within his dreams.

Her kind heart breaking with sadness, Red looks down at the suffering soul covered in her hood, and she finds herself hoping that he'll be okay. Hoping that the forest won't have cost him his life, as it almost claimed hers.

Then, as she starts to leave, she notices something else. Something strange. In the far corner of the room, hidden behind the door of the closet, is a pair of boots, black and covered in mud. Not fashioned for a woman, and too large to belong to the old man.

Her eyes squint with mistrustful curiosity, but she leaves it be.

At least for now.

Lightning flashes fiercely through the window, and the cabin creaks against the wind, as the stranger is left to sleep alone.

CHAPTER SIX

"**A**re you hungry, dear?"

Touching her hand against her empty stomach, feeling the weakness in her bones, Red nods, and Ruth moves swiftly over to a cabinet, pulling a piece of bread from within it.

"Here, take this," she says, handing it to the girl. "I am sorry that I cannot offer you anything fresher, but this should quell your hunger until tonight."

Red bites into the bread, nothing more than a stale roll, and yet to her hungry mouth it tastes as though it had fallen down as a blessing from the sky above. She looks to Ruth with thankful eyes. "What happens tonight?"

Ruth smiles. "Dinner. A feast for my guests."

Enjoying the bread and looking over to the barren dinner table, Red nods, feeling her rumbling stomach once more. "That sounds great."

"I'm glad," Ruth says. "It will be fun to have company such as yourself for a change."

In the far corner of the room, the old man grunts. "Waste of food."

At his words, Ruth's demeanor suddenly changes, and anger flashes in her eyes as she looks to the old man. "Excuse me?"

Yet, even at her anger, he doesn't back down. "It's a waste of food. It's not like we have much to spare."

"*We?*" Her voice grows harsher. "When is the last time you provided food?"

"Not fair," the old man grunts. "Tricked."

"More like incompetent," Ruth snarls. "And if I want to have a feast for my guests, that is what I will do."

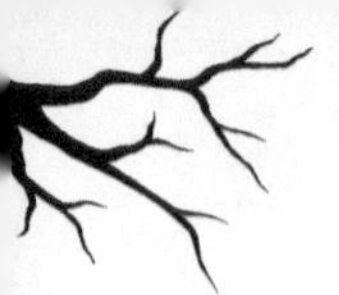

The old man groans like a beaten dog but finally backs down. Something about Ruth's tone seems to have frightened him; in truth, it frightens Red as well.

But then Ruth turns her attention back to the girl, kindness returning once more. "Sorry about that." Her eyes cut back to the old man. "Even old friends can get cross sometimes."

Red nods, but her expression betrays how uncomfortable she is. Something about their argument seemed wrong, as if it were about more than food, as if they were discussing past wounds and hidden skeletons right before her eyes.

Deep down, however, Red wonders if the source of her sudden unease is not their exchange but her own secret memories, the trauma that her mind associates with harsh words and biting tongues, and she finds herself wishing she hadn't given her hood to the stranger so she could sink within it, hide from the world around her, pretend it doesn't exist.

Yet, as she thinks upon her own past, she hears the whispered grumblings of the old man, still fighting the argument already ended.

"*Incompetent.* Cursed is more like it. Privileged *brats.* Walking over *me.*"

The venom in his voice causes Red to grow nervous once more, and she moves towards Ruth, intending to

ask what the whispers are about, hoping the answer will calm her mind.

However, she is stopped dead in her tracks by the sound of a body hitting the hard wooden floor, and in an instant, she knows where the sound has come from.

The stranger's room.

Kneeling down on the floor, hunched over, the stranger clutches his sides, feeling the bones trembling within. His breathing is still hoarse, as if each breath taken tore his lungs, and his body still shivers violently, as if it had never been the rain that was causing him to freeze.

At the edge of the doorway stands Red, looking in at him.

Pain fills his voice. "Where?"

Red moves closer, concerned, unsure of how to help him, yet feeling as if she should. "What?" she asks, confused.

Behind her, Ruth enters the room, eyeing the man with curiosity.

"Where am I?" the stranger asks, agony choking the life from his words.

"You're in a cabin, in the forest," Red says, kneeling down to his level, speaking the words gently. "We found you collapsed outside."

"How long?"

This time, it is Ruth who answers. "A few hours ago. After the sunrise."

The stranger closes his eyes, appearing tormented, holding his head in his shaking hands, but as he does, Red notices something off about the way he moves.

The way his fingers twitch.

Finally, he speaks again. "Shouldn't be here."

"You would have died out there," Red says softly, attempting to move closer to him, to help him in some way. But the moment she takes a step, he backs away suddenly, shaking his head.

"Shouldn't be here."

Then, moving almost in desperation, he pushes past them, escaping the small room and heading straight for the cabin's door, all the while Ruth's words of warning ring out behind him.

"You can't leave in this storm."

"Take my chances," the stranger replies solemnly.

"Don't be foolish," Ruth says sharply, and the stranger hesitates for a moment, looking out through the window to the forest as if he knew it would mean his death. Still, he does not move from the door.

Red moves closer, pleading with him. "You'll die. Is that what you want?"

The stranger grinds his teeth, holding the door tight, fighting the urge to open it, to leave this place. But

something holds him back, some hidden instinct keeping him here, even as his bones cry out to leave.

Something in the girl's eyes. Telling him to stay.

For what reason, he does not know.

The door shuts, and the stranger remains inside, closing his eyes as though it were a grave mistake.

"I'll stay till nightfall."

Ruth smiles. "Excellent. I'll set an extra place at the dinner table. You must be starving. You're all skin and bones."

In a distant corner of the cabin, the old man grunts.

"Should have let him die."

Thunder cries out once more, and rain mixes with the swirling wind, crashing against the walls of the small cabin and trapping the living inside.

For this night is far from over.

CHAPTER SEVEN

The fire softly burns beneath the chimney, sparks of amber light drifting off into the air, glowing bright for a moment, yet withering away to ash before even beginning their descent to the cold floor.

Still, its warmth reaches them.

The old man sits in his creaking chair, staring at the rest of them in harsh silence with uncaring eyes. Red sits upon the small couch of green, its fabric old and worn, faded cloth contrasting the bright glow of Red's emerald eyes and the dark velvet crimson of her hood, now shrouded around her once more.

The stranger rests opposite her in a chair carved from oak, now covered in loose, ragged, yet dry clothes, unwillingly passed down from the old man.

Illuminated by the burning fire, Ruth serves them tea, its steam rising up from each cup, her gaze focused on the stranger.

"So tell me," she inquires, "what brought you out to this forest in the first place?"

The stranger doesn't respond.

"It's just," Ruth continues, "it has been a long time since I've had a single visitor. To get two in one day… I thought perhaps I was missing something."

No response.

"You didn't come looking for the child, did you?"

Still the stranger remains silent, yet his eyes betray a restless soul, staring intently at the floor, tired lungs breathing heavily.

"He can't be looking for me," Red says. "I've never seen him before."

"Quite right," Ruth responds, but her tone suggests that perhaps that wasn't the answer to her question, and after a long moment of tense silence that follows, the stranger finally speaks.

"I didn't come looking for anyone."

Smiling, Ruth pours a cup of tea for herself before resting upon the couch beside Red, tilting her head at the stranger. "More curious is your arrival, then. I've not known many to come into this forest unless looking for someone."

The stranger meets her insinuating eyes, and for a moment, not a word is spoken.

"Perhaps, then," Ruth continues, "you are running from something. Like Red was. Forced into the forest by a monster on the hunt."

The words spark horror in Red's heart, and she instinctively reaches down, feeling the bandage still wrapped around her leg and the blood that has begun to seep through it, staining its white cloth a darker shade of crimson than even the hood itself.

"But, no, that won't do either," Ruth says, shaking her head. "If something was chasing you, you most certainly would not have been so eager to leave this cabin. Which means that, regrettably, you must be running from *someone*."

Shifting in his seat, the stranger flinches, almost imperceptibly, and his words echo out in a hollow tone. "You could say that."

"So, who is it, then? Who in your life was so bad that you came out here to the woods to escape their company?"

The stranger returns to his silence once more.

"What I want to know," the old man suddenly says, "is how on this rotting earth did you drag yourself through this forest in the middle of a thunderstorm?"

A flash of fierceness appears in Red's features. "I did."

The old man scoffs, waving her off. "You were afraid of something, body foolish with fear. Besides, you look to be in good health." His cold stare turns to the stranger sitting across the cabin from him. "Whereas you appear as though you died years ago. So, I ask again, *stranger*, how did you get here?"

The stranger groans, growing tired of the old man's questions. "I walked."

"Sure you did," the old man scoffs. "Just like I'm sure you came *alone*."

"How else would I have come?"

Slowly, the old man leans forward, imposing despite his age, as unspoken accusations fill his tired eyes. "Maybe more came with you. Maybe you are just the first to arrive. Maybe you're after something."

"What would I be after, in this place?"

"Revenge, perhaps."

Ruth outstretches a gentle hand to the old man's shoulder, attempting to smother the growing fire in his heart. "Calm down."

Her plea goes unheard as sharp words echo from the stranger.

"Only the guilty fear revenge."

The old man growls. "Only the foolish come to this forest."

"Enough!" Ruth finally snarls, putting an end to their quarrel before composing herself once more and speaking kindly to her old friend. "There is no point to this nonsensical chatter. Our new friend has found us, in need of help. His reasons for being lost do not truly matter."

The old man glares at the stranger but bites his tongue.

Ruth nods with authority before turning to the stranger herself. "I do have one question, though, if you will permit it?"

The stranger nods.

"How you moved through the forest, I do not care. However, I am curious as to how you found this cabin. The girl was chased here by a shadow, but few find this cabin unless led to it. So I find your appearance here strange."

As lightning flashes beyond the cabin's walls, the stranger closes his eyes as if reliving something. Some memory locked away inside his head.

"I don't remember much. Just running. Then the storm."

Red listens with curiosity, remembering how she ran herself. Blood from her wound finally escapes its bandage

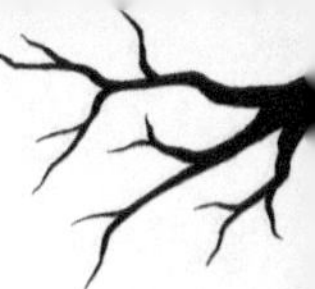

and begins to trickle down her calf, painting it in streaks of burning crimson.

"I remember falling," the stranger says, opening his eyes, which appear glassy, confused, and he speaks the words as though he can't breathe.

Thunder shakes the ground.

"Then… then I remember something. A trail."

Ruth recoils in shock. "A trail?"

"Yes." The stranger nods. "It was carved into the trees. Markings that led somewhere. I started following them." His eyes close, and his body shivers. "Then I woke up here."

Ruth chuckles, her demeanor changing slightly. Something he said has struck a chord within her, but what it is she does not say, instead merely forcing a smile. "Quite the tale."

Then, excusing herself, Ruth stands up and moves to the kitchen, intending to pour herself another cup of tea. Still sitting in the creaking chair, the old man grumbles, closing his eyes and beginning to sleep.

No longer distracted by the stories being told, Red feels something warm cascading down her calf and reaches for it. When she lifts her hand back up, red blood like ink stains her fair skin. Quickly, she tightens the bandage around her leg and wipes her hand on her crimson hood, watching as the blood vanishes within in its dark red velvet.

As she finishes, she notices the stranger watching her.

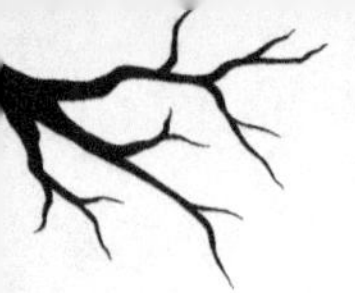

"How did that happen?"

Red glances up to him for a moment, but then her eyes find the wound once more. "Last night. Something in the forest…"

"Something hurt you?"

Red nods.

"Are you okay?"

"Yes," she replies. "I'm fine."

"You shouldn't be out here, kid. Not in this forest. Not alone."

Wincing at the pain, Red nods again.

"Can you walk?"

"Yeah."

"Then you should go," the stranger says, his tone suddenly deathly serious. "Leave this place while it's still daylight."

At the mere suggestion, Red instantly moves back, receding into her hood. The forest looming outside can be heard even from where she sits: the cracking of branches, the howl of the wind, it causes her to shudder. "I can't. There's a monster out there."

"There are monsters in here too, kid. They just do a better job of hiding it."

Red's eyes widen as she looks to the stranger: almost dead, having appeared out of nowhere. Soon curiosity overtakes her thoughts, until their conversation is stopped by the sleeping whispers of the old man.

"*The child. Mine. Took it.*"

For a moment they both eye the sleeping elder with disturbed expressions, but no further words escape his slumber, and finally, the stranger continues. "You should go, kid. Go back to your family, or whoever you're searching for."

The mention of family stabs at Red's fragile heart, and she looks down to the floor, almost ashamed. The stranger notices.

"You didn't come here looking for your family, did you?"

Red shakes her head but still will not look at him.

"So, I'm not the only one trying to escape from something."

Red's hands move slowly down her arms, as if feeling past wounds that are no longer there yet still hurt all the same.

Again, the stranger notices. "Your family?"

Nodding slightly, Red echoes his words. "Some monsters are better at hiding it."

The stranger sighs and offers her a consoling expression. "Does the old lady know?"

Red shakes her head. "No."

"Well," the stranger says, looking at her as if he could feel her pain, "your secret is safe."

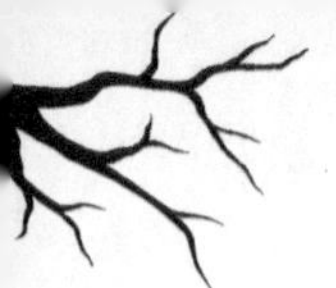

Thankful, Red nods as she pulls the hood ever tighter, a reflex learned from her youth, from all the nights she spent in that hood, pretending that the world beyond it didn't exist, that the pain, the cruelty, was just her imagination.

Pretending they couldn't reach her in the hood.

Once again, the stranger notices and appears to understand, offering a sigh of remorse. "Don't run forever, kid."

Red nods, wiping a tear as it falls down her cheek, trying not to think of the past. Trying to forget what she's run from, what's been done to her, hating herself for being so afraid. She's always been afraid. Fear is what kept her there so long, resigned to her torment, allowing herself to endure it, for fear of escape. Finally, she had enough courage to run, but here she finds herself again, hiding in a cabin, terrified even to step outside the door.

As she shivers in sadness, the old man begins to grumble in his sleep again, not even woken when the swirling wind lifts branches from the dirt and slings them against the cabin's walls, the impact felt by those inside.

Listening to the storm, trying to forget her own past, Red has an idea. "How long have you been here? In this area, I mean."

"A long time," the stranger answers. "Why?"

"Well, it's just… Ruth said she came here looking for her sister. I thought maybe you might have seen her."

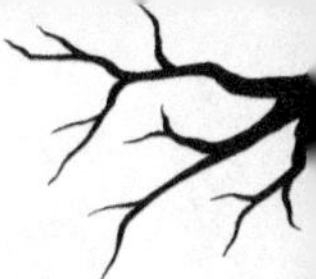

Something changes in the stranger's tone. "Sister?"

Red nods, and the stranger looks over to the kitchen for a moment, eyes focusing on Ruth. For a split second, something flashes in his eyes, and he flinches. But whatever it was, he dismisses the notion soon enough and answers Red's innocent question. "I haven't seen anyone around this forest in years."

Lightning suddenly cracks across the sky, and the old man grows restless. "*Child*," he whispers in his sleep. "*Took it.*"

Thunder echoes, and rain crashes against the windows. "*Harlot. Promised. Gold.*"

Red and the stranger look to the old man, growing uneasy, disturbed by his vicious tone, until suddenly he wakes up screaming.

"*Took the child!*"

Absolute silence follows as they stare at him in terror, and he stares back at them with harsh eyes, only now realizing that he screamed as he awoke. They wait for him to say something further, to explain his haunting words, but he never does, instead returning to his slumber, grumbling as he drifts off.

"Should have left them outside."

CHAPTER EIGHT

As rainfall crashes against the windowpanes, distorting the image of the forest lying just beyond it, Red steps into the small kitchen to aid Ruth, who is struggling to reach sugar on her top shelf.

"Thank you, child," Ruth says, pouring the sweet crystals into a steaming cup of warm tea and raising it

to her mouth with an old, shaking hand, drinking in its warmth.

Nodding, Red looks over the cabinets, noticing with a heavy heart how barren they are. Aside from a few pieces of bread and a handful of sugar, there isn't much food at all.

"It's been tough," Ruth says, seeing the young girl's solemn gaze. "Living out here. Been times I thought I would starve." She reaches over and kindly adjusts Red's bright hair, smiling at her. "But I've made it. Whenever I've lost hope, a blessing has always come along to help me get by."

"Is there anything I can do to help?" Red asks, genuine in her words.

"Thank you, child, but I'm all right. Besides, we will have food for dinner tonight."

Ruth reaches over and kicks a wooden box resting on the floor. "Found a stray lamb wandering these forests not too long ago. It will provide for us tonight."

Red looks at the small box of faded wood and then back to the living room, where the stranger still sits, smiling as she does. "He seems kind."

Ruth sneers. "He is a liar."

Taken aback, Red focuses her gaze on the old woman. "Why do you say that?"

A distrustful look covers Ruth's face as she peers over at the stranger.

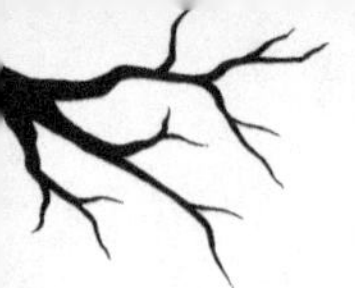

"He claims that he found this cabin by way of a trail. But I have lived here for decades and have seen no such trail."

"Perhaps it is a new one?" Red ventures.

Ruth does not yield. "Or perhaps he is lying about his true intentions here."

Concern enters Red's voice. "What other intentions could he have?"

"I don't know, child," Ruth says solemnly. "But when someone lies to conceal their past, it has been my experience that their past is never kind. Either way, I don't appreciate it when someone whom I've let into my home lies to my face."

At those words, her gaze turns to the young girl, and Red recoils in shame. It is as if Ruth were calling her out on her own lie, without having to speak the words, and the silence hangs in the air for a moment, Red feeling ashamed of the lie, yet far more ashamed of the truth.

Yet, as she feels trapped, unable to speak, the moment of quiet tension is shattered by the sudden echo of a voice that breaks through the rain, through the thunder.

A voice calling out from within the forest.

PART THREE:
THE WOMAN MISSING
HER HAIR

CHAPTER NINE

From within the forest, within the raging storm, a frail voice calls out, echoing a desperate cry for help through the trees.

"Where are you?"

In shock at the sound of another, something else living within the woods, whose very shadows portray death

itself, Red turns towards the voice's origin. Yet through the small kitchen window, all she can see is the storm. The pouring rain, the cracking lightning, all so violent that they blot out the dying trees within their drenching cloak, shrouding the decay in a downpour of torrents so that only the storm remains.

For a moment, a single moment of doubt, Red shakes her head and turns from the window, thinking she must be hearing things. Thinking the voice was just an echo of her own past, her own frail voice calling out for help as it has so many times. Yet it has always gone unheeded, drowned out by darkness thicker than even the storm.

But to her surprise, the voice echoes again, this time heard by every living soul within the cabin's small walls of wood.

"Please, where are you!?"

At the sound of the voice's plea, the sign of another trapped within these twisting trees, Ruth turns, and for a split second Red sees something flash in the old woman's eyes. A glimmer of hope, perhaps. As if, for only a moment, Ruth had dared allow herself to dream that the voice calling out was a still-living echo of her own past. Her sister, finally calling out to her.

But the hopeful glimmer in her eyes fades as quickly as it came, and the beautiful fantasies of grief are once again overtaken by the grisly, nightmarish reality.

Red, however, feels the tragic plea crawling over her bones, stabbing at her heart as she realizes that even though it is not a secret memory calling out to her, it reflects the cries of her younger, broken self all the same, and in this forest, in this storm, the voice's cries for help will go unheeded just as hers always had.

Deep down, Red might have understood why cries for help went ignored, why the righteous never seemed to intervene against the twisted machinations of the wicked, for fear that they themselves would become lost within the monster's cruel, unforgiving grasp. However, she has not forgiven them the trespass, has never forgotten those who saw her bloodied cheeks and splintered bones and simply passed on. Once, long ago, she promised herself that if she ever heard the cry of another, ever heard echoes of death escaping from those whose lifeblood was slowly decaying, she wouldn't turn away. That she would help them, no matter the cost.

She promised herself she wouldn't be afraid.

So, lifting up her crimson hood atop her head, she moves closer to the door, ready to face the storm and find the voice, save it from the forest's haunting grave.

But as she moves closer, Ruth's confused words call out behind her.

"What are you doing, child?"

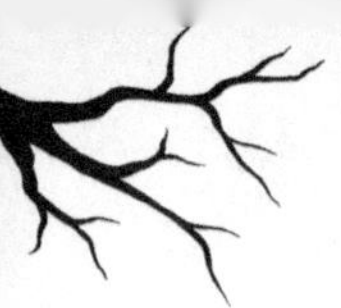

"She sounds as if she needs help," Red responds, unable to hide the quiver of nervousness in her voice.

Ruth looks out the small glass window once more and solemnly shakes her head. "I don't disagree, but look at the storm."

Outside, in only the last few moments, the storm has increased in ferocity. Thunder crashes down over the land, shattering the bark of hollow trees into dozens of jagged shards with its mere echo. Wind lifts up broken, splintered branches from the ground, slinging them through the air like flocks of ravens, talons ready to cut anything that moves.

"If you go out there," Ruth implores, "you won't make it back. Besides, there is no way to know if the voice is close to us or merely echoing from the trees."

Red shakes her head at first, dismissing the notion of leaving the voice to die, remembering the promise she had made to herself, unwilling to break it. But as she opens the door and faces the storm, she hesitates at its severity.

Rain tears through the door, so quick and so fierce that it almost cuts her skin, like silver daggers falling from the sky, drawing blood from the land beneath it.

Still, she tries to force herself to move through it. To help the voice in need.

As no one had ever helped her.

"You'll die, child," Ruth begs. "Please do not go."

Red tightens her fist, biting her lip in terrified frustration, feeling the fright coursing through her blood, knowing that it won't allow her to leave this place of safety. Knowing that after all these years, she has been lying to herself, that her promise was broken before she even uttered it.

"What if she needs help? Like I did?" Red asks, talking more to herself than Ruth, one last effort to try and bury the fear down below in the recesses of her mind where it can't hurt her, even while the rain stings against her skin.

Sorrowful words echo as Ruth puts a kind hand across the young girl's shoulder. "Then she must make it to the cabin."

A single tear of unbearable sadness falls down Red's cheek as she closes her eyes in shame, knowing the truth about herself, even if they can't see it. Knowing that it isn't the storm but the fear that keeps her from answering the cries for help. The fear of the lurking monster who's drawn blood. The fear of what it might cost. Her own life.

Red's heart breaks as her promise is shattered.

Knowing she is like all the rest.

Those who never helped.

Yet while the voice no longer echoes, no longer carries pleas of desperation through the trees, the call for help still rings within the cabin, and in the corner, seeing Red's tear, the stranger speaks.

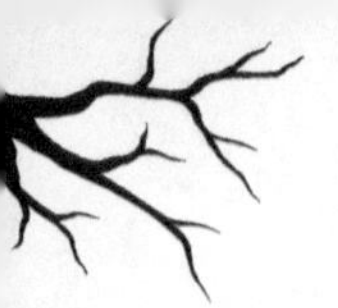

"I'll go."

"Don't be foolish," Ruth says.

The stranger ignores her warning, merely walking to the door, willing to face the storm to find the voice, if not for their sake, then for Red's, to deny her more pain than the scars hidden behind her hood have already inflicted.

A moment before he steps out, Red looks into his eyes, tears of regret filling her own, and she speaks with a grieving voice of gratitude.

"Thank you."

The stranger returns a slight nod of sympathy before he steps out into the storm, vanishing within the rain.

CHAPTER TEN

Rain falls from the sky of darkened grey, violently crashing into the stranger as he searches for the voice, and the woman it belongs to.

Mud begins to creep over his feet as he moves, like quicksand trying to bury its victims down within the earth itself, below the monstrous roots that crawl over the ground, into the grave it has made for them. The grave where their screams will be silenced, where their skin will rot and leave behind only skeletons, another set of bones for the forest to feast upon. Another life trapped in the cold dirt that has become its home, never to escape.

Still, he continues to fight its grasp, remain above the dead and among the living as he searches, hearing the voice echo through the trees that trap them both.

"Where are you!?"

The voice is soft, barely cutting through the storm's haunting whistle or the moaning agony of dying branches, but still it echoes in the stranger's ears as if it were right beside him.

Eyes cutting toward the sound, he progresses through the twisting maze of endless trees, as the piercing rain cuts across his eyes and the ferocious wind attempts to knock him over, take away his footing so that the forest can consume him.

In the distance, the pleading voice calls out, ringing in his ears.

"Where are you?"

Jagged branches, caught by the wind and sharpened by the lightning, crash into the stranger as he walks, the force enough to cut into his back, ripping his clothes and

causing him to stumble, having to reach out and steady himself against a black tree of brittle bark.

But still he progresses, fighting against the raging cloudburst, letting the voice guide him where his vision has failed, through the maze of rotting, mutilated branches that twist in upon themselves to blot out the sky. Rain pours from above, drowning out the life within it until the thicket is as barren as the grey clouds themselves, watching from the sky like death's reapers, witnessing the living souls ready to be harvested by the forest's silver scythe of steel.

Yet through it all, the voice calls out once more.

"Beloved!"

Finally, the stranger catches the fainting glimpse of a figure within the terror. The shadowed outline of a woman, shaking from indescribable horror, looking hopelessly to the forest as she cries out.

The stranger watches her for a moment, a helpless soul lost in this nightmare, who still believes this place holds hope, holds anything more than monsters hungry for blood and haunted trees forced to witness the slaughter.

Then the figure outlined beyond the rain turns and sees him as well, the shadow of another that she has found, or perhaps that has found her.

At once and without thinking, the woman runs to him, not stopping to call out, nor even look to his features, as she pushes through the storm, through the thunder, to embrace him in warmth, wrapping her shaking arms tightly around him so as never to let him escape her sight again as her tears of joy mix with the falling rain.

"I thought you were lost to me forever."

The stranger says nothing, only waiting for her to discover the truth.

When at last she notices his silence through her own wishful relief, the woman looks up, seeing him clearly now through the storm, and she recedes from her embrace, a haunting look of sorrow drowning out all traces of life from her face as more tears mix with rainfall. Only they are no longer tears of joy but tears of mourning.

"You're not him."

"No," the stranger answers.

"Who are you, then?" she asks, sniffling in sunken sadness.

Lightning flashes in the sky.

"No one."

As the two strangers stand in silence, a whistling whirlwind grows around them, scattering withered leaves and wretched branches, as the trees themselves seem to move, to grow, seeking to enclose the trapped souls within their wicked grasp, unwilling to let anything escape the evil atrocities the trees themselves are forever forced to witness lest they be forced to suffer alone.

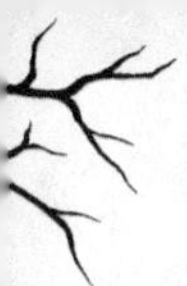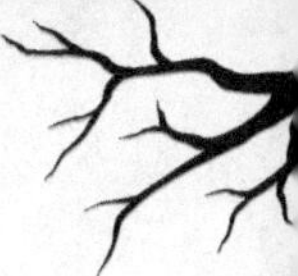

"Come with me," the stranger says, stretching out his hand. "There is a cabin."

The woman shakes her head, desperate. "I can't. I have to keep looking."

The stranger can feel her sorrow, the stabbing agony of her heartbeat, yet he speaks the dreadful truth all the same, knowing what it is asking of her.

"If you die in this storm, you'll never find anyone."

A final tear falls like rain from her mournful eyes, but although her heart screams from the depths of her soul, begging her not to abandon her beloved to this fate, and the trees seem almost to reach out to her, calling her back into their depths, she finally relents. Taking the stranger's hand, she allows him to lead her through the storm, towards the safety he spoke of: the cabin that lies within the forest.

Unaware that safety is only a cruel lie...

CHAPTER ELEVEN

ithin the confines of creaking oak, as violent rain is heard rapping against the fragile windows of glass and sharp, ragged branches fall down against the roof above, Red paces the floor, concern staining her face like a scar. She hears the thunder roar beyond the

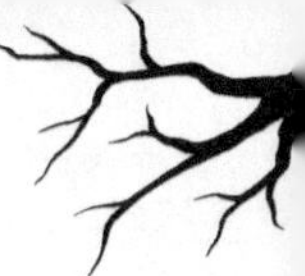

safety she rests in and fears for the lives of those trapped within it.

"He's been gone for too long."

"There is nothing we can do, child," Ruth says, walking up to Red and giving her a gentle grin, hoping to ease the miserable melancholy echoing in the young girl's nervous movements. "I warned him not to go."

The old man sneers from his seat in the corner, still not bothering to even look to the door, as if he had been certain of the outcome from the moment the stranger entered the forest. As if the thought of entering into this storm were more evidence of death than even a blood-stained corpse would have been.

"Blasted fool," he says. "Going out in this storm. Deserves what he gets."

Red glares at him with a fire in her eyes brighter than the embers that lie in the fireplace, yet she says nothing, only pacing the floor quicker, growing restless, stealing glances out of the windows, praying to see the stranger's return. To know that she didn't send him to his death just because she was afraid to go herself.

But the more she watches the storm raging outside, the more the horrible truth comes into focus, constricting her lungs and stealing the light from her eyes. The truth that, through the pouring rain, she can barely see the trees nearest to the cabin, mere feet away, and even then, it is

only as outlines in the mist, twisting shadows revealed through the rain, yet whose features are imperceptible through it. Unless the storm let up, Red would not have been able to see the stranger if he were dying right in front of her. Even now, he might be screaming for help only ten feet away, seeing the cabin's presence looming in the rainfall, not understanding why no one has come to help him, why they cannot see his pain through the storm. And in that moment, Red trembles in haunting sorrow, realizing that for all his faults, the old man is right.

If she can't see the trees right in front of her, then sending the stranger out to find a single voice that echoed in the distance was like digging his grave deep within the earth and lowering him into it. Watching as he fought to climb his way back up to the light, even as the solemn tombstone of grey fell inwards, down into the depths of the sunken hole of shadows, trapping the stranger there forever. Into the dirt where she sent him.

Yet, even while she still paces the floor in tragic, mourning sorrow, a knock echoes on the door, signaling the life that has survived the storm.

Before the knocking's echo even leaves the air, Red opens the door at once, and every living soul within the cabin steps back in shock as they see who stands on the other side.

The stranger, ragged and bloodied but still alive, and beside him, the woman whose voice they heard calling out for help, shivering from the rain's freezing chill, yet still with breath in her lungs and life in her eyes. But as Red sheds a tear of unfathomable relief, the others' expressions grow wary.

"You survived the storm," Ruth says, voice almost cracking in disbelief.

"Not right," the old man says, suddenly shaking his head back and forth, unwilling to accept it. "Not right."

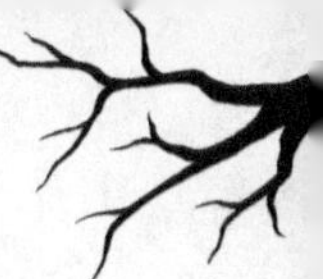

CHAPTER TWELVE

In a small chair of faded white sits the woman who'd called out for help, dry from the rain but still shaking, clothed in a once-beautiful dress of violet sapphire, now torn asunder and covered in dirt, a tragic reflection of something that once glowed as bright as the dream of a fairy-tale fantasy, now reduced to its mirrored nightmare.

Atop the woman's head is a veil, its purple velvet far darker than the dress, and it wraps tightly around her head, clearly revealing her grieving face but hiding her hair from sight.

"Have you seen him?" she asks, her question directed at Ruth, who rests in front of the fireplace, feeding it a log for its fire.

"No. I am sorry, but I have not."

Desperate, the woman describes the one she seeks. "He is tall, dark hair. Dressed like a prince."

"I'm sorry, dear," Ruth responds, "but I'm afraid it is not a matter of description. I haven't seen anyone at all in this forest in years. Least of all a prince."

"Perhaps you heard him calling out?" the woman begs, seeking something she knows they cannot give her.

From his chair in the corner, eyes cold with uncaring malice, the old man grunts. "We ain't seen him. Let it go."

Ruth shoots him a glare. "Hush, now." Then, with kindness, she looks back to her new guest. "I am truly sorry, my dear, but he is correct. We have not seen the man for whom you search."

The woman hides a tear, brushing it across her trembling cheek as she turns her hopeful gaze to Red, who sits on the weathered couch in front of her, and as she does, Red feels a tear welling in her own eye.

She wishes she could tell her that she'd seen her prince, that it would be okay, help make the woman's pain go away,

yet all she can do is return the same expression, a slight shake of her head revealing the truth, forcing more life to leave the woman's eyes.

Yet the woman remains hopeful for one last moment, until the stranger, leaning against the cabin's wall, shakes his head as well.

Fingers trembling, holding back an ocean of tears, the woman looks to the floor with grief-stricken eyes.

"He'll die out there, if he's alone."

The gravity of her words chokes out the air for a moment, until finally Ruth breaks the unspoken mourning by collecting the pot of steaming tea and offering it to the woman. However, the quick movement causes the woman to recoil in sudden shock.

At first, the rest of them think nothing of it; she was merely spooked, lost in her thoughts and not ready for movement so close. But then Red shifts in her seat, so gently it's almost imperceptible, and yet the woman jumps again as if lightning had struck the very chair in which she rests.

"Are you okay?" Red asks.

"Yes," the woman answers, calming herself. "It's just..."

The cabin creaks slightly, and once again, the woman flinches. The color leaves her eyes, and for a moment she appears as though the shock had stopped her horrified heart, stolen her soul and left an empty shell in its place.

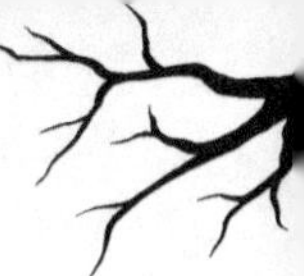

Fretful concern enters Ruth's soft voice. "What is it, dear?"

The woman visibly tries to stop her hands from shaking as she looks to the ground, embarrassed of her fear.

"It's the movement, the sounds. I'm not used to them."

The old man leans forward, interest finally piqued. "What do you mean, you're not used to them?"

She starts to answer, to reveal the secret behind her fright, but the words won't come out, as if speaking them would make the pain worse.

Finally, she manages to calm herself enough to accept the tea, thankful for its warmth. But the porcelain cup shakes in her trembling hands, and every time lightning strikes, every time the cabin creaks, every time the rest of them even take a breath, the woman flinches as if every sight or sound were a new, terrifying sensation.

Eventually, she finds the strength to look to the stranger.

"Thank you for finding me."

The stranger nods, but as he does, he looks over to her. His keen eyes see something the rest of them do not: faint stains of blood across the skirt of her violet dress that even the rain could not wash off, as well as the charred edges of the bottom hem, which fire had singed but not burned.

Yet he says nothing of it, as Ruth begins to speak once more.

"Why were you in the forest?"

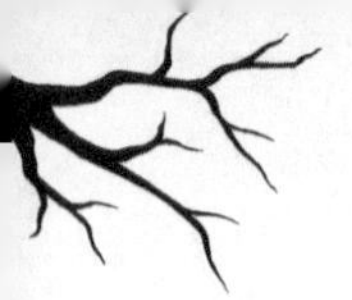

"Searching for my beloved."

The stranger's eyes remain focused on the stains of blood. "Why was *he* in the forest?"

Once more, the woman starts to speak, but hesitation steals her voice. There is a flash of sadness in her eyes, followed swiftly by a glimmer of madness. However, the former overtakes the latter, and a tear streams down her cheek.

For a moment, Red's eyes meet hers, and they hold each other's gaze, as if they somehow understood each other's past, each other's pain.

The woman notices Red holding her crimson hood close.

Red notices how the woman rubs her arms, remembering past scars.

"He…" the woman begins, finally finding the strength. "He was in the forest because he tried to save me."

"From what?" the stranger asks.

A shiver crawls over her skin. "My prison."

Save for the storm, all is silent as she recounts the tale of her life, and the horrors of her prison.

"When I was a child, my family crossed a woman. Stole something from her. Food to keep themselves from starving. But the woman found them and threatened to take their lives as payment for the stolen food, as recompense for their grave trespass against her."

The woman's bones shiver from the memory.

"I still remember her face. Old, worn down. A monster. I thought she was going to kill them, kill my parents, take them from me. But then… then they made a deal."

Tears stream down her face.

"They traded my life for theirs. Their *own* daughter. I don't know if they knew then what the woman was. I hope it would have mattered."

"What was she?" Red asks.

Dread echoes in her voice. "A witch."

Memories rise from the buried trenches of terror within the woman's mind, and in her eyes, she sees herself, a young girl with bright blond hair and skin not yet scarred. A bony hand with the grip of a serpent takes hold of her wrist, dragging the girl through a dark, evil door and into a frightful fate whose horrors she could never have imagined in her most twisted nightmares.

"She locked me in her tower, to punish me for what they had taken from her."

The crying girl is dragged up the spinning staircase, so black only its haunting spirals can be seen, so lifeless it is as if nothing else existed within it.

"I didn't see light, or hear another sound after that day."

Cries of fear and pain swirl through the never-ending spiral of sinister stairs, and as the girl is dragged up them, closer to the nothingness atop them, it feels as though she is

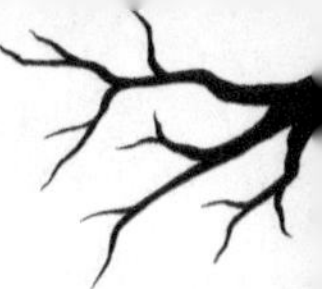

descending down, into the depths of the earth, a spinning pit of torment leading ever further into the abyss of cruel madness which lies in wait for her.

"Except when she'd come. To torture me."

In a sudden violent action so abrupt that it takes the air from her lungs, the spinning stops, the ascension to darkness over, and the girl is thrust into an empty room with a single window, a faint momentary reminder of the light that she'd once known, as her torture begins.

"I still remember her laughing."

The tower looms above the land, distant cackling echoing from within it, and the light from its single window fades from view. Yet still, the cackling remains, echoing into the present, where even they who rest in the cabin can faintly hear its maniacal melody of madness.

The woman brushes away tears, closing her eyes, attempting to block out the noises, block out the memories of dark silence, knowing nothing but her own screams as shadows inflicted unspeakable acts upon her.

Finally, she manages to calm herself and continues her tale, as those listening grow more cautious with every word she speaks.

"Then one day, he came. A prince, standing outside the tower. He'd heard me crying, even from afar."

A smile grows on the woman's face, genuine for the first time.

"We talked for months. He told me stories of what lay beyond my prison. Stories of the things I'd long forgotten. Finally, one day he climbed the tower, intending to rescue me." A tear of happiness falls. "When first I felt his embrace, he told me he would take me for his wife, and that I would be a princess, free from that horrid place forever. And for a moment, just a moment, I believed it was possible."

The woman's eyes go hollow, and she flinches in sudden unseen pain.

"But she found us. The *witch*. She shrieked as she cursed my prince, causing thorns to bury themselves into his eyes, taking away his sight."

Her voice cracks, and she shuts her eyes tightly once more.

"Then she pushed him out of the window. I heard his *scream* as he fell. Until finally the screaming stopped, all at once. I… I thought he was dead."

As the woman cries, Red reaches over, placing a gentle hand on the woman's shoulder, careful not to frighten her as she attempts to provide a momentary comfort.

"What happened next?" Red asks.

The woman's eyes suddenly flinch wildly, and her head twitches in a strange manner, both violent and calm at the same time, and as the stranger looks to her, he notices another flicker of madness behind her eyes, born in isolation and bred by torment.

"The witch punished me again." Pain rings in her voice. "She held me down and ripped the hair from my head. At first, I let her, just as I always had before. But… but then I remembered his cry, the screams of the one whom I loved, and I couldn't take it. Not anymore."

A soft chuckle escapes the woman's heart, but she buries it immediately.

A deathly serious tone rings out in Ruth's voice. "What did you do?"

The woman's eyes twitch once more.

"She killed the witch," the stranger answers, but the woman shakes her head.

"No, no, no. I *burned* her."

Ruth recoils at once. "You what?"

"I burned her," the woman repeats, something hauntingly close to satisfaction echoing in her words. "She wouldn't die otherwise. I had to. I had to stop the laughing."

They all look at her in horror.

"It was right, wasn't it?" she asks, all traces of sanity leaving her. "To stop the laughing?"

No one dares speak a word. Even the storm calms itself for a moment as the woman speaks to herself in the silence.

"Had to stop the laughing."

Then, all at once, the spark of madness fades from her eyes, replaced by overwhelming sorrow as she begins sobbing.

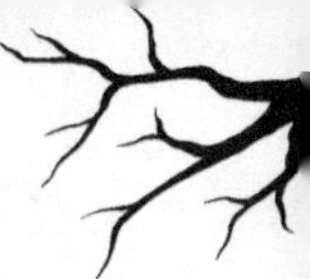

Red moves closer, trying to comfort her.

The stranger stays silent, feeling sympathy for her, yet still he stares at the woman as if something were very wrong. As if they had trapped themselves inside with someone they should not have.

Ruth, however, is less subtle with her horror.

"You *burned* someone alive? How could anyone be that cruel?"

In the corner of the room, the old man snickers. "I misjudged you, girl. Burned someone alive. Most princesses I've known won't even dirty their nails, the stuck-up harlots." He laughs for a moment. "Burned the witch. Don't hear that every day."

"Why not just leave?" Ruth asks, paying no mind to her old friend's cheerful snickering. "Why not run?"

"I don't know," the woman says, Red having calmed her somewhat. "I just… I had to."

"You did the right thing," the stranger says. "If you'd left her alive, she would have found you."

Ruth stands appalled. "You don't know that."

Solemnly, Red looks to her, trying to help her understand. "They always find you."

Silence grows within the cabin, even as the swirling wind whistles in the distance, until finally the old man chuckles.

"Did the prince die?"

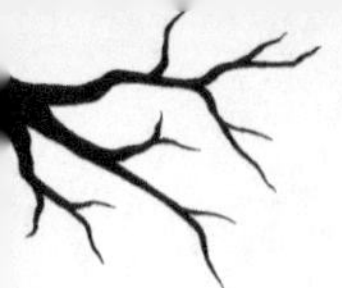

"No," the woman answers. "Once I climbed down the tower, I found the spot of grass where he'd fallen, but it was empty. In his agony, he must've walked away, into the forest."

"At least the story had a happy ending," the old man grumbles. "The prince got blinded for his arrogance."

The cabin's guests look to him in shock. Even Ruth has a level of disgust on her face as she stares at the cruel face of her old friend.

"How could you say that?" the woman asks, tears welling up in her eyes.

"What? Am I wrong? The fool climbed a tower and thought he could kill a witch. Full of undeserved pride, just like all the other princes and princesses in this land. Walk all over us when the only thing special about them is their birthrights."

"He wasn't like that," the woman says.

"Sure he was. Most of them can't even keep their word. Save them from a hanging, and can't even give a single gift in return, can't even keep a promise."

At the increasing rage building in his words, the rest of them look to him with a curious expression, and he suddenly shifts in his chair, realizing he's said more than he intended. Yet still he growls a final time.

"You ask me, we should blind the whole lot of them."

A spark of violent madness flashes in the woman's heartbroken eyes, but Red holds her close, calming her

to the old man's harsh words, until finally the woman just sighs.

"At least he's not blind anymore."

Red nods, and the rest stay quiet, allowing her that one single sliver of light that remains. Except for the stranger, who eyes her more curiously.

"What do you mean?" he asks.

"I killed the witch," she says. "I broke the curse. He's not blind anymore."

No one else says a word, for they either do not know the truth or have no heart to tell her. Even the stranger holds his tongue, but soon she notices his saddened expression.

"What is it?"

The stranger tilts his head, unsure of how to say it, unsure if he even should, or if he should let her cling to the false hope for as long as she could. "It's only…"

"What?" she asks again.

"If you killed the witch…" His voice trails off, and finally he sighs, choosing the truth. "If you killed the witch, you didn't break the curse."

Tears begin to stream down like a waterfall. "No… no, that's not right."

"I'm sorry," the stranger says, "but once a witch casts a spell, the curse can only be broken by her. If she's dead…" His voice cracks, and his eyes twitch slightly. "If she's dead,

then the curse will follow him until death. Can't escape it. No matter what you do, you can't escape it."

Unable to believe it, the woman clenches her fist in anger. "You're lying!"

The stranger looks down, face full of sorrow. "I'm sorry."

"You're lying!" she repeats, unable to breathe, begging for it not to be true. "You're… you're…"

The words won't leave her mouth, and she weeps uncontrollably.

CHAPTER THIRTEEN

"What have I done?"

Thin traces of sunlight crawl through the dark clouds rolling swiftly across the sky, twisting the once-radiant light into distorted fractures more broken than even the branches of the forest below. Still, as the once-bright glow of life is choked from it,

the sunlight is not allowed to die, forced to linger in the agonizing shadow of death behind it, mirrored by the woman in the cabin's bedroom, whose cries of mourning sorrow are illuminated by its lowly light.

"Blind forever," she recounts in disbelief, regret shimmering in her blue eyes like a memory until the cascade of witnessed blood stains them a hue of darkened velvet. "Because of me."

"It's okay," Red says gently, sitting beside her on the small cot and reaching a kind arm over to her shoulder in an attempt to console her broken heart. "It's not your fault."

The words ring softly, but the moment she feels the touch of another, the woman jumps back, afraid of beatings from her past. Soft touches, gentle words, always warping into crazed cackling and broken bones.

A tear falls down Red's face as she sees it. The same reaction she's endured countless times, the lingering scars of monsters now gone.

"You know," Red says in a sorrowful, almost ashamed tone, that of a child still trapped in the cruelty of others, "my family used to beat me too."

The revealed secret steals the woman's attention away from her own tears, and her eyes focus on Red. "What?"

Red's fingers slowly trace over her own arm, the sounds of shattered bones ever echoing in her head.

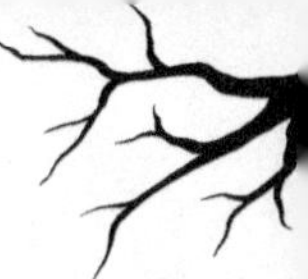

"I can still hear it. The sound of the footsteps getting closer. The waiting. Knowing what's coming but not being able to even scream."

Another tear falls from her cheek.

Lightning cracks in the distance.

"I ran away four times. But they always found me. Always."

Her body shivers as she closes her eyes and holds her hood close. All the while blood escapes from her wound, her calf stinging, though it is nothing compared to the horrors inflicted in her own home.

"I told Ruth I didn't know the stories told of this forest. But that was a lie." A hint of relief washes over her, as if voicing the truth, admitting the clandestine cruelty, healed something broken inside of her. "I've heard all of them. That's why I came out here, why I ran away to these forests. Because they've heard the legends too. They won't chase me in here. They'll let the monsters take me."

As the woman looks to Red, the grief is dampened, replaced with sympathy. She understands the girl's words far too well.

"Where will you go?" she asks.

"If I can escape this forest," Red says, looking through the window, watching the rain shower across the land, "my grandmother's house. She'll help me."

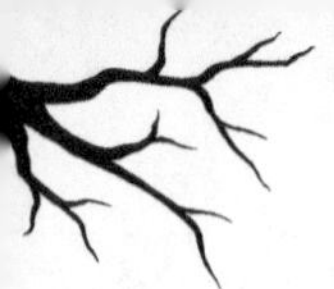

A rare smile grows on the woman's face. "I hope she does."

Red nods, brushing away a tear and sitting in silence beside the only one who's ever understood, ever known the pain, faced the haunting loneliness that echoes from it. But while the memories still linger, Red's thoughts turn back to something she saw earlier.

Something that might connect the woman's story to this cabin.

"Your prince," she asks. "What kind of clothes did he wear?"

The woman squints at the question but answers it nonetheless. "He dresses like a prince. White vest, blue gloves."

"Boots?"

"Yes. Black ones."

Red nods and stares out the window once more, uncertainty dancing in her eyes, the lingering feeling that not all is right in this place still piercing her heart.

"Why?" the woman asks.

"No reason," she says, even as the wretched thought begins to swirl in her mind like leaves in a whirlwind.

After a period of quiet calm, the woman speaks again. "Do you think he will know my voice? Know that it's me?"

Red offers a smile. "He'll know."

"At least… at least he won't see me like this."

The woman shifts her head, hair still covered by the velvet veil, eyes ashamed of what it hides.

Seeking to comfort her torment, knowing all too well that veils, like hoods, can't be hidden within forever, Red softly reaches up to remove the veil, but the woman flinches at her touch.

"No. Don't."

"It's okay," Red says, her kindness calming the woman's suffocating spirit as she gently removes the veil, revealing what lies beneath.

The woman's scalp is stained with blood, her hair having been ripped from her head, just as she had told. Only a few strands remain, small slivers of blonde left to serve as a reminder of her trespass. However, that which remains does not echo horror nor hideousness, but beauty, as it is the most radiant hair Red has ever seen, seeming as though it would glow even in total darkness.

"It's beautiful," Red says in awe.

The woman sheds a tear, nodding her gratitude, though she still hangs her head in shame, unsure if she believes the kind words of a stranger.

Seeing this, Red decides she doesn't want to be a stranger anymore.

"What is your name?" the young girl asks.

Taking a deep, solemn breath, the woman answers. "Rapunzel."

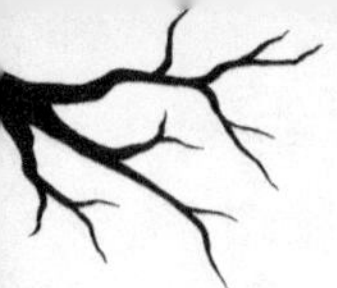

Red smiles and meets her eyes. "I'm glad I met you. Even under the circumstances."

Rapunzel nods, as if Red's presence had offered a momentary relief, but then asks a strange question. "Are you real?"

"What?" Red asks, confused.

"It's just… in the tower, alone for so long… sometimes… sometimes it's hard to tell."

"I'm real," Red says.

Rapunzel smiles. "I'm glad."

A few seconds of silence linger.

"I hope you get to your grandmother's house."

Red nods, thankful for the compassion, even if she isn't used to it. "It's funny, when I first saw this cabin, I thought it *was* my grandmother's house."

Rapunzel laughs, the first time she's done so since she can remember. "When I first saw it, I thought it looked like my prince's carriage."

"Hmm," Red sighs. "I guess we both just saw what we wanted to see."

"I guess so."

Lightning flashes. Thunder echoes.

Red turns to the closet once more, thinking of what she saw there hours ago, resting behind the door. Black boots, covered in mud.

A prince's boots.

CHAPTER FOURTEEN

"What are your intentions here?"

In the kitchen, Ruth prepares dinner: lamb roasting within the flames of the fireplace, fresh bread rising up from its dough and taking form, and a few spare vegetables, sliced neatly with a silver knife stolen momentarily from the kitchen table.

Behind her, the stranger leans on the wall, staring out with tired eyes at the all-consuming storm: the broken trees in its path, the spiraling clouds in the sky above, the rumbling of the thunder. But the visuals don't frighten him, not the ferocity of the rain or the cracking of light. It is the rotting corpse of a forest once bright that haunts his gaze, and deep down, a part of him wishes the storm would drown it until nothing was left inside. Because whatever terrors the tempest might cause, the secrets of this forest are far darker.

Secrets few live long enough to know.

"What do you mean?" the stranger finally asks, gaze still not leaving the storm.

"I mean," Ruth repeats, "why are you here? The girl was chased by something in the woods. The woman is looking for her lover. But you've said nothing of your intentions."

"I don't have any intentions here," the stranger sighs. "I wanted to leave, remember?"

"And yet here you remain. In my home, among my guests, all the while we know absolutely nothing about you." She hesitates. "Except that you are a liar."

The stranger scoffs.

Ruth returns a sarcastic chuckle. "Don't play foolish with me. You said you found this cabin by following a trail, but I have lived in these woods a long time, and I can assure you, no such trail exists."

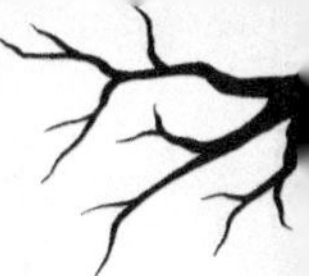

Reflections of rotting bark and twisting branches crawl into his eyes. "Maybe you don't know this forest as well as you think you do."

"Or maybe," Ruth scoffs, "you are just a liar who did not deserve to be invited into my home."

"Maybe," the stranger responds, finally looking to her.

"Tell me, then," she says while slicing through food with the sharp knife of silver, thumping loudly as it impacts the wood beneath with every stroke. "If you have no story of your past to tell, then how do you know what happens when a witch casts a spell?"

The stranger does not offer an answer.

"Oh, I think you do have a past, and an intention with coming here. I think something brought you here, some dark secret long buried. And I do not intend to place the girl's life in danger because I allowed a wolf into our midst, masquerading as a sheep."

Still, the stranger says nothing, merely watching Ruth closely as she prepares the food, as if searching for something in her movements, a mirrored reflection, an echo of something long past.

"Tell me, boy," Ruth says with a curious tone. "You've heard the woman's story, of how she burned someone alive, and seen that she was not cast out into the storm. What secret could you be hiding that is worse than that?"

The stranger meets her eyes for a moment as they both stare into one another's souls, searching for what lies beneath, unsure of whether they want to discover the truth each of them fears or leave it buried forever.

Finally, the stranger shakes his head and starts to walk away. But Ruth's voice calls out from behind him.

"Who are you running from, I wonder?"

The stranger stops, not turning back to face her, his tone deathly serious as he offers a single answer.

"Everyone."

CHAPTER FIFTEEN

All alone, Red sits on the cot, slowly rocking herself back and forth as her crimson hood covers her face from flashes of lightning that bathe the small bedroom in their luminescent glow.

Something isn't right.

Red doesn't know what, but in her bones, she can feel it. Like animals sensing a storm before the first drop of rainfall, she can feel the approaching horror rattling across the shattered pieces of her once-broken bones.

She places her hands against her head, trying to think, make sense of her dread, the feeling of wanting to crawl underneath the cot and hide from the living souls around her just as she always has before.

Secretly, she always longed to stay hidden forever, stay beneath the bed as though she were buried within it, finally free from the torment. But that was something she never dared admit even to herself.

However, something is different this time. The fear is still there, but something else has risen up within her too, like a phoenix crawling out of its prison of fire. Deep within her soul, she is tired of hiding, tired of running.

But mostly, tired of being afraid.

So, she does not hide under the bed. She does not run from the cabin back into the forest. Instead, she rocks back and forth on the small cot, replaying memories in her head, trying to discover the source of her unease.

Boots covered in mud resting in the cabin.

The harsh voice of Ruth. "He is a liar."

Red closes her eyes, still rocking, trapped in her memories.

Knocking echoing from beneath the floor.

The horrified voice of the old man. "Not right."

A carved mark left across the door.

"Not right."

Red rocks faster, heart racing.

"Not right."

The shadow that hunted her within the forest.

"Not right."

Rapunzel's broken voice of madness. "I had to stop the laughing."

"Not right. Not right. Not right!"

The door suddenly opens, stealing Red's breath as it breaks through her memories, forcing her to jump backwards in fright.

She is still shaking in shock when the stranger steps in.

"I didn't mean to scare you," he says.

Red forces herself to calm down, even as her heart still races. "It's alright." Finally, she stops shaking, but her emerald eyes remain like glass, staring at nothing at all, only thinking over the twisted clues she doesn't yet understand.

The stranger notices the unease in her eyes. "Why are you in here by yourself?"

"I just… I just wanted to be alone. To think."

The stranger nods. "Okay, I'll leave you alone. The old lady just wanted me to tell you that dinner would be ready soon."

With that said, he begins to shut the door, but Red's haunted voice suddenly stops him.

"Did you see the blood on her dress?"

The stranger nods solemnly.

"If all she did was burn a witch, there wouldn't have been blood."

The stranger sighs. "I know."

A nervous expression cascades over Red's face, illuminated by a strike of lightning. "I don't know who to trust."

The stranger shakes his head and offers a haunting piece of advice before shutting the door back and leaving her alone once more.

Even when he's gone, his warning still echoes around her.

"Then don't trust any of us."

CHAPTER SIXTEEN

apunzel saw it.

All alone in the corner room of the cabin, searching desperately as though she had gone mad, she found it. What she has been searching for. Her beloved.

Or at least, what he left her.

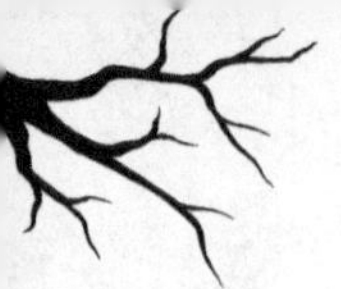

In the dark room, her fingers creep down, sliding beneath the cot and touching the leather cover that lies hidden, waiting to be found.

She'd been alone for so long, trapped in darkness, in silence so haunting it drowned out her even her thoughts until all that was left was fear, the emptiness of isolation. But then she found him. Her prince.

Now, she might find him again.

She pulls it from beneath the cot, holding it up above her, waiting for the storm's fury to illuminate it, reveal the truth she longs for.

Though in her hands, she can already feel it.

Rapunzel smiles. She knew he was close.

Lightning strikes at last, revealing the source of her hope. The remnant of life left behind, proof that her beloved was here once, in this cabin, waiting for her.

Her prince's journal.

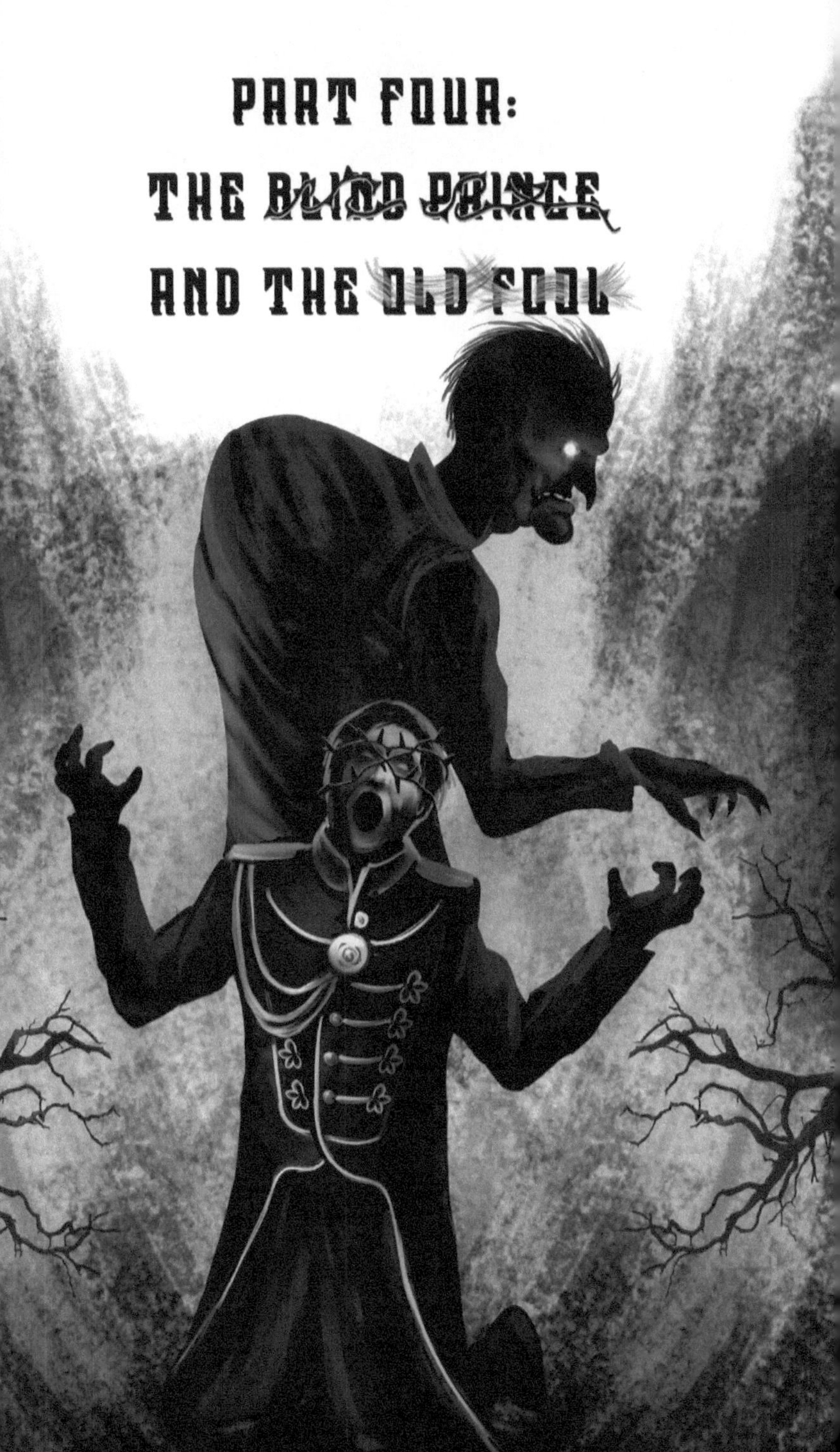
PART FOUR:
THE BLIND PRINCE
AND THE OLD FOOL

CHAPTER SEVENTEEN

A cover of faded brown leather. A latch of rusted silver. This is all that keeps Rapunzel from the truth. From the inscriptions of her prince, the secrets that lie behind his time spent in this cabin, among its guests, just as she is now. Surrounded by strangers whose intentions

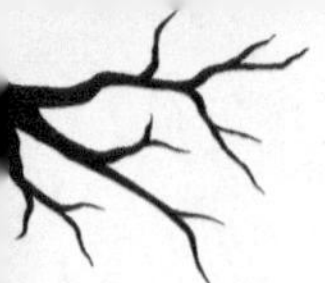

are unknown, whose identities remain shrouded in the lies told of the past.

Her eyes shimmer with reflections of what she hopes to find written within. Tales of how he survived the fall, survived the forest. Tales of finding safety in the cabin, solace in the company of those inside.

Of course, somehow, deep inside, her heart already knows the truth of what she'll find. The haunting words of a soul long departed.

Yet, just like the children who don't believe the stories told of this forest, she allows her heart to hope, pleading against the storm that the fairy tale her eyes reflect could be real. That somehow, even in the shadows of this place, they could live happily ever after.

Foolish dreams, like all the rest…

Hands shaking with frightful anticipation, hiding behind the small cot and letting the fiery cracks of lightning beyond the window illuminate the room, Rapunzel opens the journal and begins to read.

Dearly beloved,

For what feels like a lifetime, I have wandered through this forest, searching for you. Hoping beyond reason to hear the sweet song of your voice and feel your embrace once more.

If I am granted but one wish in this life, it will be that I find you here amongst the trees, calling out my name, waiting for me.

A tear gently falls down Rapunzel's face as she reads the scattered words written by a blind man, whose affliction couldn't stop the words of love from pouring out, wishing she could hold him even now, granting the wish in both of their hearts.

Were this broken world kind, had it felt her struggle and sought to ease her suffering, a bolt of lightning would have cracked in the sky, striking her heart, ending her pain before she could keep reading. Before she discovered the horrors most only dreamt of in their most twisted nightmares.

But this night is cruel, and so her suffering has only begun.

Days have passed since my last inscription, and the forest is darker than I could have imagined. There are monsters here that I cannot see, but I feel their haunting presence surrounding me all the same.

There are moments I feel fortunate to have lost my sight, so I cannot see them. So that in blissful ignorance I can imagine a bright forest glowing with life and not the barren land of death that seems to crawl over my very skin.

Whatever is here, whatever dark creature lives in this breathing graveyard, it is darker than even the witch who stole my sight.

As she reads, cracks of lightning reflect in her eyes, seeming to twist until they become remnants of the tragedy she reads, playing out in her eyes as if she had witnessed it herself: flashes of blood, of thorns and blind eyes, even a glimpse of the shadow that loomed over the prince, the eyes glowing red moving in the woods around him.

Yesterday, I stumbled into an open field and fell upon what at first I thought were rocks. But when my hands felt them, I realized the truth. They were bones, broken and decayed, hundreds of them scattered out over the land, sunk down into the dirt as if they were part of the forest itself.

I fear my skeleton might join them in the ground.

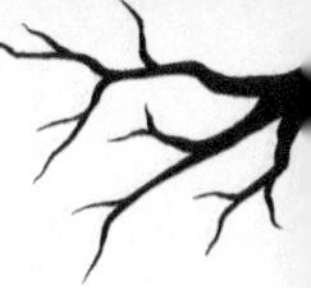

Desperation grows fiercer in Rapunzel's eyes as she flips through the pages, inscriptions describing day after day, each more haunting than the last.

It was ripped to shreds. The deer I heard cry in the night. I found its body, the flesh torn from it. But the stench remained, filling my nostrils with rot.

Something is very wrong with this place.

More tears stream down her pale skin as thunder echoes, and the faint traces of sunlight which once crept through the paned glass begin to fade as the sun sets in the sky.

Letting the darkness expand its grip over those still breathing within.

This forest is sick. It surrounds me like a rotting coffin, slowly suffocating me in it. All I feel is death. Decay. I fear that eventually I shall wake and feel my own skeleton revealed, the skin having finally withered away, leaving my hollowed skull to sink into the dirt, unable to even scream as it claims my life.

Sounds of death echo in my ears, drawing blood from them. Cries of animals being slaughtered. Howls *of monsters in the night. Days ago, I thought I heard the screams of children.*

Lightning flashes. Rapunzel jumps.

More pages turn.

I take it back! The wish I made, to find you within this forest. I have nightmares of your skull trapped among the field of bones, your voice being stolen from you as you try to cry out to me. Yet I can't see you. I take it back!

If somehow you can hear me, stay away! Please! Stay away from this place!

The journal snaps shut as Rapunzel cries, not wanting to accept there was a monster, no cursed creatures or biting bark great enough that he'd wish never to feel her embrace again, just to spare her from it. Most of all, she doesn't want to read of the death of her prince, knowing it will mean she'll be all alone once more, trapped in the darkness of despair. But curiosity is a cruel creature, and it forces her to open the book once more. And the words written reveal hope.

Light against the darkness.

But just as lightning appears beautiful for a moment, only for the lie to be revealed as its haunting power cuts into the heart of the earth beneath it, so too do these words echo a horror she cannot yet understand.

But then, I found this cabin...

CHAPTER EIGHTEEN

efore the storm. Before the girl in red ran through the trees. Before the stranger arrived, or the woman missing her hair could cry out into the forest, there was the blind prince. Wandering through the forest, blinded to its twisted visuals of distorted death yet feeling them claw at his soul all the same, he desperately searched for a way to escape.

As so many others had before him.

But time had taken his strength and sorrow stolen his spirit. Terror had scraped off every piece of the once-brave prince, leaving only a shell behind, something broken that jumped at the mere rustling of branches in the wind, and he stumbles to the ground.

Dirt covers his hands, and twisting thorns echo in his eyes, as he stays down, no longer having the strength to rise up again.

In his heart, he thinks of his beloved, of what she has endured at the hands of a monster. Trapped alone in that horrific tower, never to see light as she is tortured within it, forever in darkness just as he is now. It must be a cruel fate, he thinks, that he should die as she has lived. Alone, blinded, wishing that death would take him from his suffering.

"I'm sorry," he tells her, broken words filled with pain as he realizes he will never hear her voice again, the voice that first cried out to him from atop the tower, not begging for help but pleading not to be alone any longer. "I can't go any further. Forgive me."

In the dirt, the blind prince lies, waiting to die.

But then, a sound echoes.

At first, he shakes his head, thinking it is nothing, more cries of animals soon to be slain whirling within the withered trees. But then, he hears it again, the faint sound of someone's voice.

Hope coursing through his heart, the blind prince summons his will and stands up, desperately calling out towards the voice.

"Hello?"

No answer comes. For a moment, he pauses, but then, with renewed strength coursing through his bones, he begins to move as quickly as he can, stumbling between trees yet not willing to relent, seeking the origin of the sound. The heart behind the voice.

"Hello?" he cries out again, begging for any sign of life. "Is someone there?"

The blind prince is now running through the trees as the sound grows louder, grows closer, until he can almost hear it clearly.

It sounds almost like an argument.

"Help!" he screams once more.

In the distance, more voices echo, until finally the faint hint of spoken words can be heard clearly.

Once, many months before, he heard a voice in the distance, a kind voice begging for another, and he went to it, finding happiness he couldn't have imagined. Finding his beloved.

This time, what waits for him is not happiness.

It is a nightmare...

CHAPTER NINETEEN

"*Y*ou old fool," an old woman's voice echoes into the forest. "What have you done?"

Withered branches of dying trees seem to reach out towards the prince as he moves closer to the voices, blinded to the walls of wood in his path. The trees whose roots twist unnaturally on the ground, eternally trapping the trees *themselves, forcing them to witness the tragic tales that unfold, the screams that always echo, all while something else forces them to move against their will, grabs hold of the innocent things that enter within and keeps them trapped here, waiting for slaughter.*

Yet they do not take hold of the prince, and he moves ever closer to the sound, finally reaching a spot where no roots seem to twist.

A place the forest allows him to enter.

"I did what…"

As abrupt as a strike of lightning called down from the heavens above, the old man stops speaking, looking behind Ruth and seeing the blind prince through the window. "Who's that?"

Ruth turns, seeing the prince as well, the poor desolate soul looking for refuge, for safety, and her expression changes from one of anger to one of concern.

"Good heavens," she says as she moves to the door, stepping from her cabin home towards the prince standing outside, who appears on the verge of death, eyes without sight, pupils with no form, and covered in twisting thorns. "Are you alright?"

The blind prince breathes a sigh of relief, and his thorn-covered eyes water with unimaginable gratitude as he steps towards her, thankful that his nightmare is finally over.

But then, the raven attacks.

It darts down from the sky, a black streak of coarse feathers and nightmarish features, crying out as it flies straight for the prince, baring its razor-sharp talons as it crashes into him.

Stumbling back, the prince cries out in a panic, unable to see the feathers falling from the frenzied bird as it attacks him, digging its talons into his skin, lifting up its dark wings like death's angel and flapping them wildly.

Even blinded, the prince manages to shake the deranged bird from its attack, but it doesn't last. The raven attacks again, shrieking out at the top of its lungs, scratching the prince and drawing blood with every strike.

Trying to drag him back within the trees.

Back into the forest.

A swirling whirlwind of black feathers circles the confrontation of fallen royalty and cursed carrion, having fallen from the raven during its violent assault, and within the whirlwind of darkness, the blind prince begins to stumble backwards, inching closer to the forest, farther from the safety the cabin promises.

Until finally, Ruth manages to shoo the bird away, ending the prince's torment.

The raven flies off, back to the trees, finding a place atop a broken branch where it can lick its wounds. Yet it does no such thing, instead still crying out, ever watchful of those who stand below with its hollow eyes of pitch black, knowing more than most could even imagine.

Watching over the forest like death's reaper.

A haunting harbinger of horrors unheeded.

Falling to the ground is the blind prince, covered in bloody scratches, unable even to see what attacked him, only knowing the pain it caused and the shriek that still echoes within his ears.

"Help me," he begs. "Please."

Ruth bends down, softly taking his hand.

"Come. Let's get you inside."

CHAPTER TWENTY

A tear falls from Rapunzel's face as she faces the window, imagining where her prince must have stood when he found this cabin, stolen safety from the forest's grasp. She imagines the hope that must have filled his heart, the hope that he'd survive this place, the hope that he would see her again.

It's the same hope that still burns within her.

But then, as she looks out with joyful eyes, thinking she might find him once again and escape this forest forever, she notices something. Something dark, moving between the spiraling branches of the trees with outstretched wings, blocking out the thin traces of light from the rising moon, painting the cabin in its horrifying reflection.

Rapunzel's eyes fill with surprise for a moment, but then shock turns to terror as the raven cries out, its bloodcurdling shriek drowning out even the storm for a moment, all the while staring right at her.

Staring right *through* her.

Jumping back at once, Rapunzel shrinks down, hiding beneath the window, not wanting to see if the monster still watches her. Not wanting to accept that it is real, that it has crawled from the pages of the past detailed in the journal out into the real life that still surrounds her.

So instead, she opens the journal once more, the words of her prince ringing out as though he were mere breaths away, speaking directly to her.

This cabin is nice, and the old woman is kind. She bandaged my wounds and offered me shelter until I could make it on my own. I am afraid to hope, beloved, but perhaps I will be able to escape this forest and be with you once more.

In her heart she sees him, sleeping alone on the small cot, thankful for rest.

But something is wrong with this place as well. I hear wood cracking in the night, something echoing from below me. As I wake, I hear the breaths of the old man, watching me sleep.

She sees her prince clearly, waking from his restless sleep and taking off his mud-covered boots, which she noticed hiding in the corner, and she reads his words with increasing dread.

The old man has done something. What it is, I do not know. But it is something dark. The old woman curses at him when she thinks I cannot hear, but they never speak of it otherwise. I fear even she doesn't truly know what he has done.

Rapunzel cuts her glance to the door, hearing the voice of the old man as he mumbles to himself in the adjacent bedroom, most likely talking in his sleep.

A spark of madness flashes in her eyes before she starts reading once again.

I heard it, in the dark. I heard the old man speak his name.

Sitting alone in the small cabin bedroom, where his beloved would sit days after, the blind prince furiously writes in his journal, terror coursing through every stroke of the pen.

If I die before I can escape his grasp, let this be a record of his crimes. He is the one they are searching for in our kingdom. The monster the king's guards still hunt for to this very day.

Footsteps echo behind him, and the blind prince writes faster.

He is the one who turned straw to gold. The one who made the princess promise to give him her only son in return.

The cry of a raven echoes in the night.

He is the man who broke into her home when the princess wouldn't give him the child as she had promised. The man who slaughtered the boy in front of his mother, out of revenge or anger, or perhaps both.

Shaking, the prince trapped in darkness feels his heart stop in his chest as he writes the haunting words, his shaking hands forcing the strokes to come out wild, frenzied, even as he himself cannot see them.

I must get out of this place. I must get away from the monster. I pray I can convince the old woman to come with me, lest she also die by the monster's hand.

In the dark room, someone looms over the prince.

Even now, I can feel his presence. I can feel his cold breath creeping across my skin. I do not think I am alone.

A final footstep echoes, and the prince turns to face the monster.

From the prince's eyes, all he sees is nothing, an endless void of absolute black, yet still he knows the truth of what is there.

The old man looms over him, crazed look in his eyes, murder in his heart.

From outside the cabin's walls, the struggle can be heard, echoing death into the forest. It is over within a moment, and again a raven cries out in the distance.

Then, all goes silent.

Tears stream down from Rapunzel's eyes as she reads the final words inscribed in the journal, the final pen stroke stopping suddenly before the death ensued.

The last warning her prince could give her.

The monster's name is Rumplestilt

The journal falls from her hands, and she cries out, sobbing alone in the small room. In her despair, she doesn't even have the strength to speak a word of denial as grief consumes her entirely, and she wails in uncontrollable pain on the cabin's floor.

Dead. Her prince is dead.

Slaughtered in this very cabin where he searched for her, *because* he searched for her. Had he left her in the tower, had she not cried out, he would have been safe. Spared the torment of darkness that she had known, spared the dread of death, the pain of dying.

It was because of her.

Now, weeping on the floor, she feels that compared to the pain of losing him, knowing how he died, the memories of torture from the tower seem to pale in comparison.

Through all she has endured, she has kept a single spark of life, of hope burning within her. But now that he is gone, murdered in the forest because he cared for her, that spark is gone too, and she is left hollow.

Until something else takes its place.

As the tears finally stop, something else flashes in her eyes. A spark of the new fire that burns inside her, not of fear or even madness.

A spark of anger.

CHAPTER TWENTY-ONE

ries of Rapunzel's sorrow echo through the cabin, filling Red's heart, and she moves to go to her, offer comfort if she can. But she is stopped by the soft touch and gentle words of the old Ruth.

"Let her grieve alone, child. She has been through much. More than she even knows."

Red turns, surprised by the words. "What do you mean?"

Looking down for a moment, Ruth sighs solemnly. "I lied, child. I have seen her prince. In fact, he stayed here for a time, as you have."

The young girl's eyes grow wide, not out of surprise that the prince stayed there—the boots revealed that to her—but out of shock that Ruth is confiding in her.

"Where is he now?" Red asks.

The answer comes in a saddened tone. "I do not know. One morning I woke up, and he was merely gone. Vanished into the night. I hoped it was because he had heard his princess calling out his name, but now I realize it was just a fairy tale I told myself to hide the truth. He must've gone back out there, to his death."

Upon hearing the truth, Red's heart breaks in two for Rapunzel, imagining the loss she must've already felt, searching for a prince she wouldn't find.

"Why didn't you say something?" she asks.

Shaking her head, Ruth answers. "I told myself it was to spare the young woman pain, but really, I wonder if it was out of shame. I should have protected him, made sure he stayed out of the forest. I shouldn't have left him alone, in his condition."

Eyes watering, Red looks down in shame. She had been mistrustful of Ruth, thinking she was a liar because

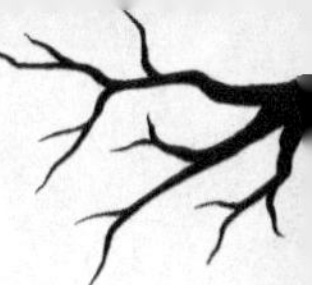

the boots remain. But still, Ruth confided in her, and so Red offers a consoling smile.

"It's not your fault. You couldn't make him stay."

Ruth reaches over, touching her hand. "Thank you, dear."

Finally, Red looks back over to the small room, where the crying has suddenly stopped, replaced by the haunting silence of loneliness. "Should we tell her?"

"No," Ruth answers as lightning flashes and a raven cries. "She is already scarred. I fear what the truth might do to her."

CHAPTER TWENTY-TWO

You've heard this tale.

The girl in red, running from the beast, bloodied and bandaged, begging for the forest to spare her life. The princess, stolen from her home and locked away in a dark tower, tormented by a wicked witch, never to

know the light of day or the song of life. You've even heard of the old man with an amazing gift but a sinister heart, someone so callous that the life of a child means nothing other than vengeance fulfilled.

Yet the stories told only focus on the escape. The girl in red finding refuge from the monster, the princess with golden hair fleeing the tower that locked her away. Tales of tragic terror cut short at the first moment of happiness, or escape, leaving images of a beautiful life dancing in the hearts of those who hear it.

Beautiful life.

Beautiful lie.

Because the aftermath of the horrors runs too deep. The scars of cruel intent, the hearts warped by fear and rage until the mere feeling of empathy is but a memory, carved out until hollow and replaced with only insanity, where even grief can no longer reach them.

That's when the true tragedy comes out. Not when the innocent souls are stolen away, not when they are tormented by monsters of the night, but when they escape. Because in truth, it isn't them that escaped, not really. No, their light is left in the place where they first discovered the darkness, and all that crawls from it are the broken pieces formed from the remnants of the monsters they faced.

Living things whose eyes flash only madness.

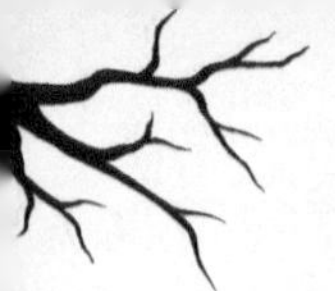

Yet still there is hope. Of light rising up once again, of the madness fading from their eyes, so long as nothing more is stolen from them.

But something has been stolen, in this very cabin. A life, a love, a way out of the darkness, the somber hope of a happy ending.

All that remains is echoes of death.

The cabin lies within the trees, forever a part of the forest, barely visible from the light of a rising moon as rain drowns the sky and thunder shakes the ground beneath.

Within the creaking walls are the strangers trapped by the storm.

In the kitchen, Ruth readies the food: preparing meat in the fireplace and baking what little bread she could from what's left in the barren cabinets.

The stranger looks out the window, watching the storm, the falling twilight left from the setting of the sun, as his hand twitches slightly.

In the corner of the room, Red rests in a small chair, wrapped tightly in her crimson hood, memories of harm dancing in her thoughts, even as the rain crashing down above provides relief, numbing the sounds around her, making her feel as though she were alone, safe within her hood.

But past the kitchen, past the living room where the guests now lie, is a hallway, small and narrow, and beyond it is a bedroom where someone is fast asleep.

The old man lies on a cot, grumbling in his sleep.

Unaware of what looms over him.

Someone watches him from the shadows of the room, inching their way closer as the old man moves restlessly, yet he is not awoken. The shadow moves closer still, until it is right over him, watching him sleep, studying every breath he takes, the thin traces of a life soon to be stolen.

For what feels like a lifetime, it stares into his soul.

Heart racing as it imagines what is to come.

Finally, the old man wakes up, groggy at first, hazy eyes barely making out the figure of a shadow before him. But then, as his vision finally returns, he sees Rapunzel standing over his bed, silver knife in her hand, flashes of rage in her eyes.

In his foolishness, the old man scoffs. "What do you think you're—"

His words are cut off as the blade slices his throat.

Instinctively, he reaches up to stop the bleeding, but the blood has already been spilled. No sound escapes his mouth even as he tries to cry out, eyes of evanescent color growing dim as he falls back onto the cot, dying in silence.

Alive one moment, dying the next, just like all those he'd killed in the kingdoms beyond, and in this very cabin.

If nothing else happens, still his recompense will have been served.

His death assured by the blood pouring from his flesh.

But the madness flashing in Rapunzel's eyes burns bright, visions of past trauma stealing her sanity.

A girl locked away in a tower.

Her grip tightens on the knife.

A witch ripping hair from her skin.

Her eyes flinch with unkindled fire.

The old man killing her prince.

Once more, Rapunzel lashes out, not willing to let the old man die in peace, instead stabbing him in the chest, once, twice, thrice, over and over again as lightning flashes, and thunder hides the sound of her attack, not stopping until both she and the room are covered in his blood. When the old man breathes no longer, when the lightning quells and the thunder's reprieve can no longer hide the sounds of her slaughter, she drops the knife, and the madness leaves her eyes.

A room of blood that can do nothing to spare her pain.

Alone, she falls to the floor, crying once more.

CHAPTER TWENTY-THREE

Outside the bedroom stained in blood, Red hears Rapunzel cry once more.

At first, she thinks to leave it alone, allow her to grieve in peace. But then she looks to the bedroom curiously, noticing something. Slowly her eyes glance over to the bedroom where Rapunzel went before, where she sat with her for a time, before moving her gaze back to the room where the woman now cries.

Two different rooms.

Curious, Red goes to investigate, followed closely by the stranger.

Knocking once, she receives no answer in return, and left with no other choice, she slowly opens the bedroom door, intending to do nothing more than comfort a friend in need.

Until she sees the slaughter…

The sheer sight of blood covering the room forces her to scream, but the sight of the old man's corpse keeps the voice from leaving her throat. For that twisted moment, surrounded by crimson as though it had fallen like rain within these walls, she stands there in complete shock, not yet able to understand.

Behind her, even the stranger's weathered eyes widen in horror.

It's then that they hear the sobbing once more.

In the corner of the small bedroom painted red, Rapunzel sits on the floor, gently rocking back and forth, covered in the old man's blood.

Disbelief rings out in Red's words. "What did you do?"

"Had to," Rapunzel says, eyes glassed over. "Had to kill the evil."

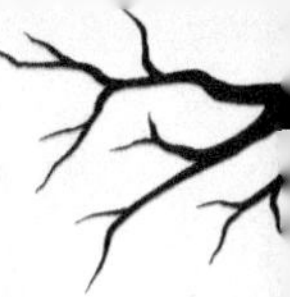

The stranger steps over to the body, smelling the blood, the corpse left behind.

Rapunzel looks up to Red, her veil removed, faint traces of once-beautiful hair now covered in crimson as she speaks to the only soul her heart still calls friend. "Had to kill the monster."

Backing away, Red's breath begins to fade. "Why?"

"Found the journal," Rapunzel says, her voice angry yet hollow. "He killed my prince. Killed a child."

Red backs away further, confusion and terror spreading across her face.

Tears streak down from Rapunzel's eyes as she looks to her friend, not wanting her to be afraid. "Prince left me a message. Told me who the old man was. What he had done."

Finding the lone journal resting on the ground, the stranger kneels down to lift it up, opening its leather to look inside, as Rapunzel's words still echo.

"Had to. Monster."

The stranger sees what was left inside the journal, the message inscribed, before his gaze turns to Red, his eyes filled with dread.

"Left message," Rapunzel recites. "Killed my prince."

Unable to stop her instinct, Red looks to the journal, heart stopping as she sees what is written within it.

Nothing.

Every page is blank. Every last one.

Slowly, the truth of the matter comes to light.

Red's sorrowful eyes turn back to Rapunzel, a part of her not wanting to tell her the truth, unsure if the broken thing can bear any more pain. But finally, she does.

For what else can she do?

"It's blank."

The crying stops for a moment as Rapunzel tilts her head in confusion. "What?"

"It's blank," Red repeats reluctantly.

Color vanishes from Rapunzel's eyes as she grabs the journal for herself, wildly flipping through the pages. "No... no... can't be. It was here."

She holds the journal up for them to see, a final effort to deny her insanity as she begins to cry.

"It was here... it was..."

Lightning flashes through the cracked window.

Not a word is spoken as the collection of poor souls stand in silence, looking over the bloodied remains of what was once the old man.

Finally, the haunting quiet is broken by Red. "What do we do?"

No answer comes.

Rapunzel covers her head in her hands, attempting to hide from what she has done, trying to wipe the blood from what hair she has left. The stranger only stares at the

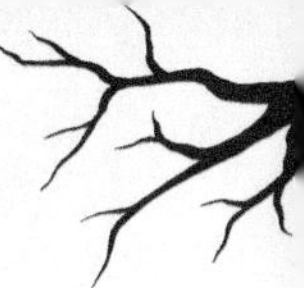

body as if all he'd known was horror and this was merely another stain of blood witnessed before his eyes, yet no less haunting because of it.

"We can't let Ruth see this," Red finally says, looking to the stranger. "She can't see this. It will kill her. And if not, she'll throw Rapunzel out in the storm."

She looks to Rapunzel, shedding a tear as she sees her rocking on the floor, remembering how she was not willing to brave the storm to spare her life. How for as long as Red could remember, fear of her own torment stopped her from protecting others, even from protecting herself, and in this moment, whether it's just or not, she can't find it within herself to allow Rapunzel to be subjected to the forest's cruel tempest nor its hunting creature.

"She's not well," Red says. "But she doesn't deserve to die. Not by the beast that's out there. We have to protect her."

Hearing her pleas, the stranger takes a final deep breath, eyes looking to the corpse, then the empty journal, and finally the storm raging outside, now lit by the glow of a rising moon. At last, he makes his decision.

The girl is right. They can't send Rapunzel out into the forest.

For the monster is growing near…

Finally, he speaks. "We hide it."

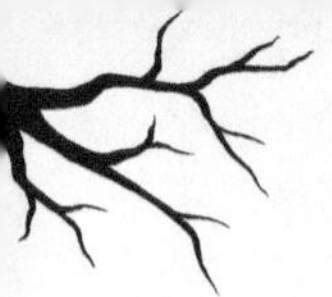

"How?" Red asks. "We can't go outside without Ruth seeing."

Branches crash against the cabin as the wind whirls and whips outside.

Closing his eyes, knowing the sinful act it suggests, the stranger speaks. "Under the floorboards."

For a moment, all three of them look down to the floor, expressions of dread covering their faces, until finally the stranger kneels down, running his hands over the wooden flooring before finally taking hold and ripping a board from its place.

Suddenly, the crazed look of lingering insanity leaves Rapunzel's eyes, and she sheds a single tear. "I'm sorry," her broken voice says to no one at all. "I'm so sorry. I didn't mean to."

"Take care of the blood, however you can," the stranger tells Red as he rips another piece of wood from its place, splinters flying as he does. "Flip the sheets and try to wipe it from the walls."

Red moves to try, but the sight of the old man's body keeps her frozen as Rapunzel's voice begs from below her.

"Where is he?" she asks. "If the journal's blank, then what happened to him?"

Unable to go nearer to the body, instead Red moves closer to Rapunzel, comforting her, yet remaining cautious.

"He was here," Red tells her, trying to ease her pain. "Ruth told me. But he left one night. He's out there in the forest somewhere."

"He's… he's still alive?" she cries.

"Yes. He's still out there somewhere, probably looking for you right—"

Her words are cut off when the stranger jumps back from the floor in shock, staring down in horror at the opening he has created.

The sudden fear in his eyes paints the picture more clearly than any amount of blood ever could, yet not a word is spoken as Red and Rapunzel move to the opening and peer down into the dark crevice within the broken floor, jaws falling, eyes widening as they see what the stranger has unearthed.

Down beneath the floor, beneath the broken wood, rest bones.

Ribs, spine, skull. All of it human.

All of it dead.

But the true source of pain is not the mere sight of bones. No, the thing that made Rapunzel unable to breathe, unable even to think, is the skull itself, thorns covering the holes where its eyes should have been.

Cries of indescribable sorrow wail from Rapunzel's broken spirit, unable to control it yet unable to deny what her eyes have seen.

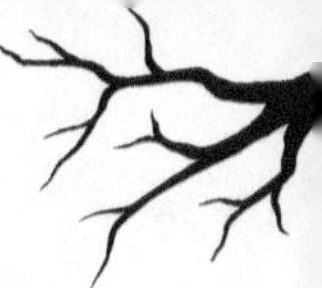

So too does Red stare down into the hole dug beneath the floor, at the skeleton resting there, her heart not willing to believe it until finally the shock is broken, replaced by a haunting look of realization.

"So… the old man did kill the prince?" she asks, confused. Her gaze turns to Rapunzel as she finds herself breathing a sigh of relief, thinking that at least the slaughter was justified. That is, until the stranger speaks, nothing more than a whisper, too quiet for anyone else to hear.

"The journal was still blank," he says. "Which means she is still not well."

"But then," Red asks, "how did she know?"

The stranger shakes his head. "I have no idea."

In the corner, rocking on the floor like a child listening to a delightful melody only she can hear, Rapunzel sits, reaffirmed in her actions. "Killed him. Deserved it."

Ignoring Rapunzel's descent back into madness, Red pleads with the stranger. "We have to make sure Ruth doesn't find out. If the old man really did kill him, we can't let her be thrown out into the storm to die, even if she's not well."

The stranger appears as though he is not fully convinced, but still he nods, not willing to throw her to the monster that feasts beyond these walls. It's then that he begins moving the old man's corpse into the floor, hiding his body from sight next to the victim he took.

While the corpse is hidden, Red looks to Rapunzel, trying to get through to her, force her to understand the gravity of what is happening. Force her back into reality, no matter how painful the reality might be.

"We can't tell her, okay?" Red says, staring into Rapunzel's eyes. "We have to act like everything is normal."

"What if…?" Rapunzel says, life coming back into her eyes. "What if she asks…?"

"We say he's sleeping," Red says, knowing all too well how to act normal to avoid suspicion, how to hide horrors committed. She has done it so often, hiding scars, bruises that would have revealed the abuse inflicted on her. "We say that he didn't want to be disturbed."

"Okay," Rapunzel says, nodding slowly and taking a deep breath, holding tightly to Red.

"We just have to make it until morning," Red reassures her. "Then we can leave while the sun is out."

Rapunzel gives her an expression of unknown gratitude, suddenly hugging her. "Thank you."

Yet as their embrace calms them both, the haunting nerves of something wrong only grow in the stranger's eyes. He peers down through the crevice, into the earth that hides what lies below the cabin, and in his dread, a question arises.

"How long ago did you say you escaped the tower?"

Rapunzel looks to him, confused. "A week, maybe more."

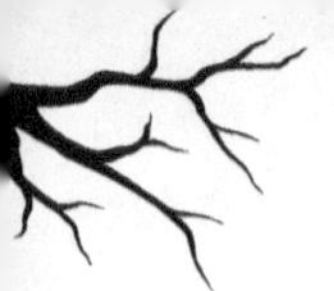

His eyes do not leave the prince's skeleton, the pile of bones left behind. "How much more?"

Still, she eyes him curiously, but she answers the question nonetheless. "No more than ten days. At the most."

The stranger stares for a final moment, uneasy about something he does not say, before closing the hole back up, hiding the horrors committed within the small cabin in the middle of the vast forest.

Surrounded by blood, silence grows until all they can hear are the faint screams of the old man, as if still they echoed within these walls, the horrific wailing like a dying animal, even though as he died no sound escaped his bloodied throat.

It's the screams of a ghost, forever trapped in the cabin where its corpse now lies, like the trees bound to the dirt by twisting roots, pariahs forever paralyzed in place, forced only to witness the dark devastation that arose from the night.

Finally, Red breaks the silence, offering a single glimmer of hope. "We just have to make it until morning."

Suddenly, the door opens, stealing away their breath.

On the other side stands Ruth, looking in at them, her shadow outlined only by the candlelight softly burning behind her.

They stay frozen in fright, knowing that blood still covers the wall, still covers Rapunzel, so much that it could

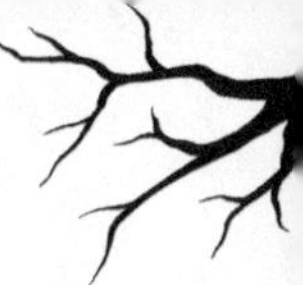

never have been washed away, waiting for Ruth to cry out in terror, to wail in agony over the murder committed.

But she never does.

"Forgive me," she says, "my vision is not what it once was. I can't see anything in this darkness. Are you in here, child?"

Shaking, surrounded by crimson, Red answers in a trembling voice. "Yes."

"Excellent," she exclaims. "Well, come out at once."

Ruth offers a kind smile.

"Dinner's ready."

PART FIVE:
THE DINNER

CHAPTER TWENTY-FOUR

The table is set.

Lit by the glowing embers of a fire burning bright in the fireplace behind them, the food covers the large table of wood, a feast prepared for the cabin's guests. A few loaves of bread rest in a bowl, an assortment of vegetables spread out over the remainder of the feast: carrots, potatoes, a

few ears of corn, yet even they pale in magnificence compared to what lies in the table's center. Displayed proudly is the lamb Ruth has spent the day roasting just for this occasion. It isn't much, but just enough for a single night.

A single dinner.

At the head of the table sits Ruth, offering gentle smiles to her guests, appearing as though her heart is overjoyed to have company as the storm rages outside. In the chairs surrounding her sit the cabin's guests.

At least, those whose bodies are not hidden beneath the floorboards.

A gentle aroma rises up from the food, warm and ready to be eaten. The guests, however, aren't feeling very hungry.

"Are you alright?" Ruth asks. "You seem a little shaken up, dear."

Forcing the lie of a calm smile, Red manages to quell the urge to scream at what they have done, whom they have hidden. "I'm fine," she says. "Just tired, I guess."

"Perfectly understandable," Ruth replies. "After what you went through in the forest, I don't know how you'd ever rest quite the same. I'm just glad I could take you in."

Closing her eyes, Red stops a tear from forming as flashes of blood paint her once-bright-green eyes a haunting shade of ruby. "I'm glad too."

Turning her head to the rest of her guests, Ruth notices no one has taken a bite yet, or even touched the food, as she prepares her own plate. "Please, don't wait on my account. I'm sure you all must be starving."

They nod their heads, yet none of them find the strength to look directly at her as they slowly start to grab food for their plates, Red still unsure of how to eat it after what they've done. Guilty hearts breed a failing appetite.

Crashing rainfall echoes down from the roof above, and for the briefest moment Red feels disconnected from the forest, as if the rain were removing it from her mind, trapping her forever in this cabin, and the ghosts crying out from beneath it.

"I wonder what is taking him so long in there," Ruth says, looking to the bedroom door where they told her he was sleeping. "Usually once he smells food he is out here before I can even set the table." She looks for a moment longer, concern slipping into her expression. "I hope he's alright."

"I'm sure he's fine," the stranger answers, without the hesitation still present in Red's quivering voice. "Just sleeping."

A small, almost imperceptible chuckle escapes from Ruth's gentle demeanor, and Red's heart stops for a brief moment, terrified that Ruth has seen through the lie.

"That old fool," Ruth chuckles. "Always sleeping."

Allowed to breathe once again, Red feels as though she can hear her own nervous heartbeat as she moves to

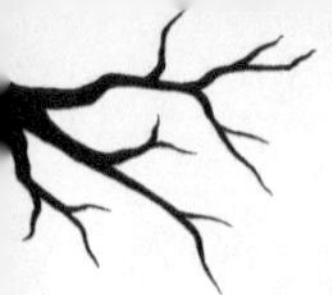

grab a piece of bread, and as she lifts it from the bowl, her hands begin to shake.

"Are you sure you're alright, dear?" Ruth asks. "You look dreadfully pale."

Red tries desperately, but she cannot stop her hand from shaking.

"Perhaps," Ruth suggests, "you'd like to go lie down?"

"No!" Red cries out suddenly, terrified of being forced back into the bedroom where it happened, where the blood still stains the floor and bones would lie beneath her feet.

The shock in her voice causes Ruth to eye her curiously, until Red speaks once more. "I'm sorry. It's just… I can't sleep during a storm."

Ruth laughs halfheartedly. "You were certainly able to last night."

Hiding her twitching hands beneath the table, Red thinks of a lie. "It was the running, I guess. Wore too much on my strength."

Grinning, Ruth responds. "I suppose it was."

Finally, Red manages to steady her hand, and she takes a bite of bread, filling her empty stomach like sweet honey, finally calming her down.

That is, until she notices the spot of blood still fresh upon Rapunzel's left sleeve. Not obvious, but also not unnoticeable, and once again, Red finds herself unable to breathe.

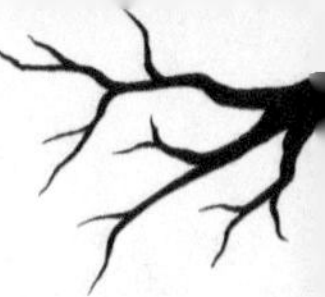

Looking out the window, Ruth comments, "Storm seems to be getting worse…"

Thunder booms in the night sky, and the wind shakes the walls of the cabin.

"If it doesn't let up soon, I fear we might just be stuck together for longer than we thought."

Rapunzel nods but shivers slightly at the implication, knowing they can't hide the slaughter forever. Meanwhile, Red can't take her eyes off the blood.

"I, for one, don't mind the company," Ruth continues, smiling as she looks over her guests. "It's so hard nowadays to find kind guests to have the pleasure of dining with."

The stranger offers a fake yet still friendly chuckle. "Kind? Here I thought I was a liar."

Ruth returns his dry sarcasm. "Oh, you most certainly are. But you are a kind one nonetheless."

A moment of silence passes as Ruth and the stranger look into each other's eyes, both appearing as though they searched for answers to questions the other guests didn't know to ask.

"What would you rather face?" the stranger asks, breaking the silence. "A kind liar, or a cruel man who speaks the truth?"

"Hmm," Ruth ponders. "An interesting question. I suppose I'd rather enjoy the lie."

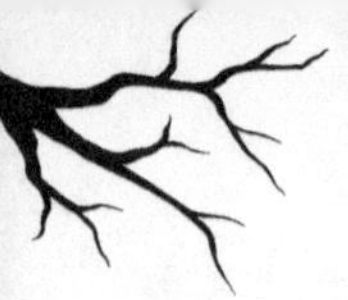

Finally, her eyes leave the stranger and she turns to Rapunzel, who has not yet spoken, too frightened that her words would reveal the truth.

"What about you, dear?" Ruth asks.

Cautiously, Rapunzel stops biting into an ear of corn and joins the conversation. As she does, her left hand rests upon the table, blood in plain sight. "I'd rather know the cruel truth. At least then… at least then you don't have to pretend."

Ruth looks to her, surprise in her eyes. Then, a look of sorrow. "Well, then, I hate to lie to you any further."

Red tries to remain calm, but the blood stained upon Rapunzel's sleeve remains visible even as Ruth stares right at her.

"The truth is, dear," Ruth confesses, "your prince did come this way, in distress. He was searching for you. I offered to let him stay, and he did for a night or two." With sympathy, Ruth looks to Rapunzel, eyes a mere glance away from seeing the blood and learning the truth of what they have done. Who they have buried. "But he left one night, without a trace. I am truly sorry. I wish I could have convinced him to stay. I wish he were here now, with us. With you."

Nodding, Rapunzel closes her eyes for a moment, visions of her prince dancing in her mind, both of the man she knew and the bones she witnessed.

"I do too," she says, pausing as sorrow chokes her words. "It's okay. I understand why you didn't tell me."

The stranger's eyes widen as he notices the blood on her sleeve as well.

"Hmm," Ruth says with a curious tone. "You took that better than I had expected."

"I guess…" Rapunzel tries to think of a lie, unease growing with every moment she pauses. "I guess I've already cried over his death enough."

"I suppose you have." Ruth nods. "Nevertheless, you have my deepest apologies for the mistruth. I know how it feels not to know what happened to someone you love."

Utter silence overtakes the room as Ruth reaches over to pat Rapunzel's hand.

The blood-covered hand.

Time seems to freeze. Lightning slowly creeps down the night sky through the window, and falling raindrops slow to a crawl.

No one can breathe.

Rapunzel still doesn't see it and is about to let Ruth touch her blood-covered hand when Red suddenly moves, lifting her own hand up, revealing the blood that now covers it.

It is enough for Ruth to notice. "Good heavens, dear!" Immediately, she stands up to grab a washcloth to wipe away the blood, and as she turns away for the briefest moment, Red looks to Rapunzel, motioning to the blood on her hand.

"It's alright," Red reassures Ruth as Rapunzel cleans her own hand behind her. "I just accidentally brushed the bandage on my leg is all."

Ruth turns back a second after Rapunzel finishes removing the bloody evidence and moves over to Red, cleaning her hand like a mother caring for an injured daughter.

"You have to be more careful, child," Ruth says. "Blood is not easy to remove. It stains, more than you know."

"I'll try."

As Red's hand is once again returned to a look of fair white, Ruth smiles and retakes her seat.

For a few moments, no one says a word, allowing somber silence to grow as they eat their meal. The stranger tries the bread as Red takes a bite of the lamb, eyes widening suddenly at how good it is.

Good enough to settle her uneasy stomach.

"It's good," she exclaims.

"Why, thank you," Ruth nods.

Rapunzel takes a bite as well, her eyes twitching slightly, putting Red ill at ease once more. "This *is* good," she says as she takes another bite. "I've never tasted anything like it."

Ruth grins. "It's the way I roast it, a little at a time. Keeps the flavor better than simply burning it all at once. You roast something too quickly, there's no telling what will happen to it."

Her eyes cut to the bedroom door once more.

"Perhaps I should wake him? I hate for him not to be a part of this dinner, as irritable as he may be."

With those words spoken, Ruth starts to get up, intending to go to the room.

The mere movement almost causes Red to jump.

But then the stranger speaks, stopping her. "It was probably difficult to fall asleep in this storm. Let the old man rest. The food will be here when he awakes."

Ruth hesitates for a moment. "But then the food will get cold."

Glancing to the door, Rapunzel feels her heart flutter in fear as she tries to think of something. "Then maybe… maybe we can put it beside the fire, so it will be warm when he awakes."

None of them move, waiting to see what Ruth will do, afraid she will continue on to the room where they told her he slept and find it empty, without a trace of life.

Red's eyes find the storm, shivering as she imagines being thrown out there to die should Ruth discover the horrible truth, hiding merely a few steps away.

Finally, Ruth grins.

"Marvelous idea," she exclaims. "A little fire is just what it needs."

A few strikes of lightning flash in the sky as she prepares a plate and places it by the fire before retaking her seat.

"So, tell me, stranger," Ruth says, "it is almost nightfall. The moon is rising as we speak. Are you still planning to leave us, or can we convince you to stay a little while longer?"

The stranger takes another bite of bread, glancing out the window.

Red notices his fingers twitch slightly, as though the bones were trying to escape his skin.

Finally, the stranger answers her question. "I guess you'll have to wait and see."

"Ohh, a mystery, then." Ruth chuckles slightly. "Well, in the meantime, I hope we can at least get some meat on those bones. You look half starved, son."

The stranger cuts his eyes to her. "You have no idea."

Suddenly, a raven crashes into the window, cracking it ever further, causing the guests to jump in shock.

For a moment it disappears, but then it cries out, shrieking into the night as it returns, raking its talons against the glass, desperate to scare those who hide within the cabin's walls. It succeeds as Red stares with wide eyes at its wretched black feathers and its seemingly empty eyes,

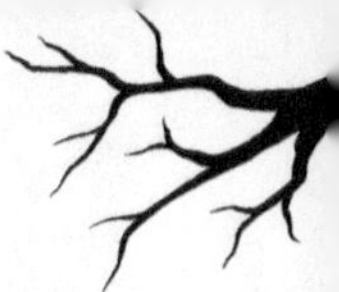

which stare right back at her as it beats its claws against the cracked window, fighting against the rain.

A frenzied, unnatural act, even for an animal trapped in this weather.

Eventually, when it can no longer fight the storm, the raven is deterred, and it flies back into the forest, haunting wings illuminated by flashes of lightning as it does, all the while still crying out.

Remnants of its broken glass and shattered silence still linger within the cabin's walls, as the guests resume their conversation and calm their nerves.

However, most of them don't notice what happened during the raven's distraction. They don't notice the empty place on the table, where a silver knife rested only a moment ago.

A knife now hidden beneath the table, waiting to be used.

"I'll never understand what's wrong with that bird." Ruth shrugs.

"Maybe it's the storm," Red suggests. "It's got everybody a little crazy, after all."

"Yes," Ruth chuckles. "I suppose you're right. Anything stuck in this storm long enough is liable to go mad."

As she speaks the words, Rapunzel's eyes flicker as if a candle were trapped inside her head, gently fighting against the wind to stay lit. Fighting to stay sane, in a world of isolation and darkness.

From the look in her eyes, it was losing.

"He's awfully quiet in there," Ruth says, taking a bite of bread. "Typically, he snores something fierce." A moment of dread passes over the rest of them as Ruth tilts her head towards the bedroom door. "Strange."

Red speaks to cut off her train of thought. "How long did you say you've lived out here?"

"What?" The old woman's eyes rest on the door for a moment longer before she turns to Red, focus now broken. "Oh, I've lived here for many years, child. It's where I grew up. I left for a time, but it was almost thirty years ago when I heard the rumors of my sister's return. Then I came back here to this place, searching for her, what was left of my family."

She looks off into the forest and smiles contently.

"I was still a young woman then." She chuckles. "Well, reasonably so."

Forcing a smile, Red hides her nervousness, even while guilt grows in the pit of her stomach.

The stranger, however, tilts his head slightly at Ruth's words, as if a thought had entered his head. A poisonous idea.

"What about you, dear?" Ruth asks, looking to Rapunzel. "Do you plan on returning home to your family after you leave here?"

"Why?" Rapunzel asks, with echoes of sadness in her harsh voice. "They sold me to a witch. Why would I want to go back there?"

"I don't know." Ruth shrugs. "Maybe to mend fences, try to bury the past."

Rapunzel lets out a sudden uneasy laugh and takes another bite of lamb, savoring every flavor. "They can burn for all I care."

The grip on the knife beneath the table tightens.

"Families," Ruth says. "A curious thing. I, for one, never thought my sister would return here, to this place, after everything that happened. And yet still, she came back home." Looking out at the storm and the forest caught within it, Ruth shrugs. "I guess for some, it is easier to burn the past than to bury it. I mean, after all, once you bury something, it starts to rot, corrupts the very land it's buried within, until everything around it smells of death and decay."

Red's hand begins to shake again. Fire burns in Rapunzel's eyes.

"Whereas," Ruth continues, "if you burn something, it's simply gone. Nothing left to… to fester, to dig up. It merely ceases to exist."

The stranger cuts his eyes up. "I suppose that's why they burn witches."

A half-hearted chuckle echoes from Ruth as she looks back to him with a piercing glance. "I suppose it is."

As Red reaches across the table to grab another piece of lamb, she notices the empty place on the table. The missing knife.

But before she can react, lightning strikes, and thunder rumbles, so fierce that it shakes the cabin once more. Only this time, the cabin doesn't return to normal. This time, the shaking moves something. A door, not closed tightly enough.

The door to the room where the bodies lie buried.

Where blood still remains.

They all stare at it, Red unable to breathe, Rapunzel's eyes twitching more wildly with each passing second.

Even the stranger seems to grow nervous for a moment as the door that hides the evidence of their misdeeds slowly creaks open.

"Oh dear," Ruth says. "I better go shut that."

Silence echoes. Red's hands shake violently, and a terrified tear streams down her face.

In that moment, they all know it is over. There is no excuse, no lie to keep her from the door. She'll see the blood. She'll scream, curse their names, send them out into the cold storm to die.

Beneath the table, the knife slowly turns towards Ruth, its sharpened blade ready to stab her the moment she rises from her chair.

She looks to the door for another moment, aged eyes unable to see the traces of blood glimmering within

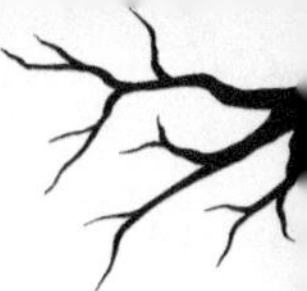

from this distance, and an eternity seems to pass for Red, trapped in terror.

The knife grows closer to Ruth.

"Well," Ruth ponders, "on second thought, I'll just close it later. I'd hate for the sound to wake him up."

Red is allowed to breathe again, trying to hide it as she gasps for the oxygen her body has been denying her. Rapunzel closes her eyes in relief, hiding the candlelight of madness burning ever brighter in her blue eyes. Even the stranger lets out a small sigh before reaching over and grabbing a piece of lamb from the center of the table.

Yet for each second of calm that passes, Red feels the truth stabbing at her heart, drawing blood from within her, staining her soul in its shade.

"It's a funny thing," Ruth says. "For all the grief that old fool has given me, I'd have to say he is probably the only real friend I have had in a long time."

Looking down in shame, Red feels her heart break as Ruth still continues.

"I know he's not a kind man, or even a clever one for that matter. But still, he's the only old friend I have left. So many others have passed on."

A tear falls down Red's cheek. Remorse even seems to break through Rapunzel's madness, causing her to look down in solemn shame, until finally Ruth speaks the words that finally break Red's soul completely.

"I don't know what I'd do without him."

Unable to take it, the weight of sorrow on her heart, Red's single tear becomes two, then three, until finally she is weeping at the table, consumed by guilt even for a crime she did not commit.

Concerned, Ruth looks to her. "What is it, dear?"

Red tries to stop it, knowing what the truth will mean, but she can't. She can't take it anymore.

"What's wrong?" Ruth asks gently.

Rapunzel looks to Red with bloodshot eyes of sorrow, begging her not to say it, not to reveal what she's done.

But Red can't stop it. Flashes of the murder ring in her head as though she were its victim, until she can feel the guilt cut across her chest like the sliver blade of a knife, drawing crimson with every stroke, and finally, her soul forces her to speak as sorrow chokes her words.

"I'm sorry. I'm so sorry. We…"

Rapunzel sheds a tear, begging her without words.

The stranger merely looks to her, softly nodding, knowing what she has to say and resigning himself to whatever outcome may lie ahead. All while he lifts up the piece of lamb, ready to quell his hunger.

Sobbing, Red tries to confess. "We… we…"

Ruth reaches over and gently touches her shoulder. "It's okay, dear. You can tell me."

Through tears and blood-red eyes, Red speaks, unable to hide the truth any longer. Compelled by her innocent heart to speak the horrific truth.

"We… hid…"

"Hid what?" Ruth asks as Red weeps.

"We hid his—"

Then it happens.

Her confession cut short by the sudden, horrified jump of someone in complete, all-consuming terror.

All at once, they look over to the guest who jumped so violently. The one whose eyes still look as though death would be a sweet relief from their current state. Who at once realized the truth they couldn't have imagined in their worst nightmares.

The stranger.

The piece of lamb falls from his hands first.

Then his entire body flinches in fear as he coughs up what he's just eaten.

"Are you okay?" Ruth asks.

The stranger doesn't answer. Doesn't even hear her. He just stares down with trembling eyes at the table, the feast, the food he's tasted, every part of his body reacting in pure, unspeakable horror.

Finally, he looks up from whatever horrific sight it is that he alone can see, and his desperate gaze finds Red. Before, in his eyes, she always saw nothing, nothing there,

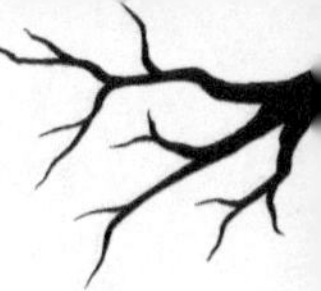

nothing left, as if the fear itself had stolen the life from him. As though his eyes had grown hollow to death, so that even in abject terror, they could reveal no true emotion. Hollowed out, so that nothing could hurt him.

The forest didn't scare him.

The storm didn't shake him.

But now, in his eyes, Red sees pure horror.

"You're shaking," Ruth says. "What's wrong?"

The stranger turns to her, part of his mind here, part of it somewhere else, entangled in the dark secret of the forest, within the very soil that lies beneath it all. Slowly his skin turns as pale as the old man's corpse, and they all stare at him for a moment longer, which seems to stretch out into eternity, as if they were watching him die motionless before them.

The moment is only broken when he stands up from the table and backs away, shaking as he does, eyes unable to leave the feast prepared, until finally he turns and moves to the room where the bodies lie hidden beneath the floor.

Red doesn't understand how he can go back there. Back into that room, where the blood still lies and the horror of what they've done still remains.

For she does not know the secret revealed to him.

The secret that causes the slaughter of the old man to appear as though it were a fairy-tale ending.

Still, those at the dinner table stare in shocked confusion, wondering what frightened the stranger, until finally Ruth speaks once again, this time to Red.

"You better go check on him," she says. "He doesn't seem well."

Nodding, Red slowly turns, sorrow and remorse having been forgotten, replaced by anxious dread as the healed bones that lie beneath her scars rattle within her, bringing remnants of old pain as if in warning of what is to come.

A warning she does not heed.

As Red walks away, leaving the final two guests alone, Ruth looks to Rapunzel, smiling, and as the old woman speaks, Rapunzel grips the knife tighter still.

"I'm sure we can find something to talk about in their absence."

Moments later, Red steps into the small bedroom, skin crawling as she enters, having no choice but to return to be surrounded by blood once more, yet it is not the dead that she now fears, but the living.

For the stranger is pacing the floor like a crazed animal caught in a snare, bones twitching, eyes flinching, maddening expression of desperation on his face.

"What's wrong?" she asks, not knowing what else to say.

The stranger doesn't answer, for the horrible thoughts consuming him do not allow for a word to be spoken.

Fighting the urge to run, Red moves closer, concern echoing in her terrified words as she pleads for an answer. "What is it?"

Finally, as the stranger stops shaking and looks out into the forest just beyond the window, he speaks, voice trembling yet firm.

"We have to leave. Now."

Confusion covers Red's face. "We can't, not in this storm. You know that." Her eyes resist the haunting temptation to look down to the floor beneath and imagine the secrets buried there. "Please, just tell me what's wrong."

Unwilling to speak it, he shakes his head and pleads with her once more.

"We have to get out of this place."

At those words, Red backs away slightly, frustrated by his lack of explanation, too afraid to imagine going back into the forest while the night's heart still beats. "We can't… we can't go back out there at night." Her voice trembles as she remembers the beast that chased her. "There is *something* out there."

"It doesn't matter. Not anymore," the stranger says, shaking his head as if in agonizing pain. "We have to go. Now."

"I won't." Red backs away further, memories of terror spreading over her. "I won't. I won't go back out there. I won't let you make me."

Almost in a panic, she turns to walk away, but the stranger grabs her wrist, stopping her in her tracks. As she turns back to face him, she starts to scream at him to release her, until she sees the true expression on his face, the weight resting within his eyes as he looks down into hers, and at last he utters the words in despair. The truth of the cabin. The secret lying within the forest.

"It's not lamb."

For a moment, her eyes flash confusion. "What?"

Horror fills every word.

"It's. Not. Lamb."

Lightning flashes. A raven cries out.

Red stands in disbelief.

"Then what…?"

Her words trail off as the truth sets in. Within seconds, her face loses every bit of its color, making her appear as though her body had died long ago, and only her ghost remained. She finds herself unable to breathe as it all hits her at once, the unthinkable truth playing in her mind in flashes of distorted memories.

Ruth's voice echoes in her head. "Found a stray lamb wandering these forests."

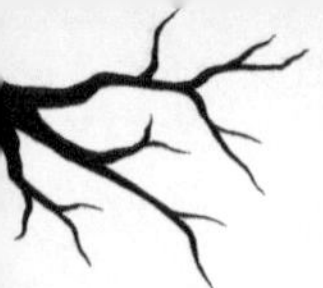

Falling to the ground in agony, Red begins to hyperventilate.

The blind price wanders the forest, finding the cabin.

Red can no longer feel the beat of her heart as it seems to stop, as her soul is stolen by the horror completely and her mind is left to scream in silence.

Beneath the floorboards lie the prince's remains.

Reduced to mere bones after only a week buried in the ground.

In the kitchen, surrounded by the raging storm, the grinning old woman watches the young princess feast.

"Are you enjoying your meal?"

Rapunzel takes another bite of what she thinks is lamb before drinking wine from her cup and nodding her answer.

"Good," Ruth says, letting out a slight cackle. "I'm glad it's to your liking."

Nodding again, Rapunzel gently takes a deep breath. The candlelight in her eyes burns furiously as she listens to the storm not soon to let up, contemplating what she might have to do to survive.

But then, Ruth says something that surprises her.

"You know," Ruth whispers, "just between you and me, I don't think my old friend is going to be joining us at all this evening."

Rapunzel swallows hard, suddenly anxious again, tightening her grip on the knife just in case Ruth has discovered the truth.

In a nervous voice, she responds, "What makes you say that?"

Ruth shrugs, but something about her is off. "I don't know. Just a feeling, I guess. You know that feeling you get in your bones when you desperately know something is wrong, but you can't tell what it is. Almost like you can feel death near you. As if it follows you."

Slowly, her gaze turns to Rapunzel.

"Do you ever get that feeling?"

Uneasy, Rapunzel responds in a quivering voice. "No."

"I do," Ruth says, shaking her head as if in mourning. "All the time."

Silence lingers. The storm rages outside. Rapunzel's hand trembles beneath the table.

"But I must confess," Ruth continues, "that is not how I know my friend won't be joining us. Do you know how I know?"

Rapunzel shakes her head.

Ruth smiles and speaks slowly.

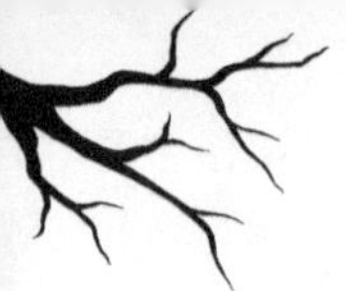

"I know he won't be joining us because in the decades I've lived in this cabin, there have been many, many bodies hidden beneath the floorboards. So many I've lost count. But do you know what's never happened?"

Ruth looks to Rapunzel, voice still kind even as her expression slowly morphs into that of something darker than even a monster.

In terror, clutching the knife for safety, Rapunzel shakes her head.

"Not once," Ruth cackles, "has one of the corpses buried beneath the floorboards ever crawled its way back out and rejoined the living." All at once Ruth laughs, so jarring it scares even the storm for a moment. "I see no reason why dear old Rumple would be the exception."

As the words of spoken secrets linger, Ruth stares into Rapunzel's eyes, watching the terror enter them.

"Poor Rumple," Ruth continues. "I wish he hadn't had to die, but unfortunately, he made a mistake when he killed the princess's son. I could have forgiven the foolish gamble he made with the woman about guessing his name. I could have even forgiven the lost meal. But what I couldn't forgive was him killing the child, and potentially leading the king's men here after him. Unnecessary risks, for nothing more than petty revenge."

As she speaks, her tone grows ever darker, matching the storm raging outside.

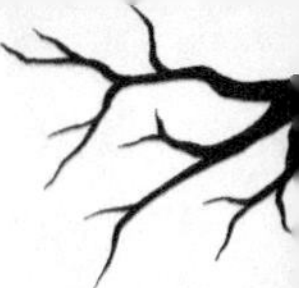

"But still," she says, shrugging, "he was my only friend. I didn't think it right for me to kill him myself. But once I saw the insanity bred in your eyes, years of isolation and torture no doubt having taken their toll, I knew you'd do it for me. All I had to do was show you your precious prince's notebook."

Tears fall from Rapunzel's face as she listens in terror.

"For what it's worth," Ruth snickers, "it's all true. I didn't doctor a single word. Well, except for when our dear stranger picked it up, that is. I couldn't let them be sure of the truth, so I cast a simple spell to make the words appear blank, just like I made that blood appear on your dress earlier. Red herrings to shift their perception, make it easier for them to label you insane."

A raven cries out once in the distance.

"It's a simple spell, really. The art of illusion. It's the same spell cast on this very cabin, making whoever comes near see what they want to see. What they hope for. Red sees her grandmother's house; you see your prince's carriage."

She laughs with madness. "The children even saw candy, if you can believe it. All lies, just the same. The siren song, the lighthouse leading only to destruction, as all beautiful things do."

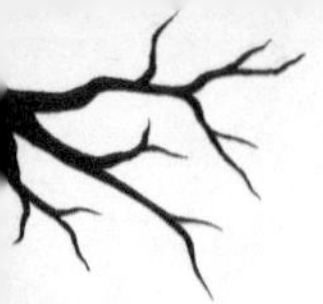

Ruth looks into the distance for a moment, out into the storm, before her mind returns to her, and she focuses once more on the notebook, the final message of the prince.

"I must say, he had remarkable penmanship for a blind man," Ruth muses, playfulness in her voice. "It's too bad his instincts were greatly lacking. But, one man's misfortune is another's opportunity, I suppose."

Another tear falls from Rapunzel's eyes.

"He screamed for you when we killed him, you know. Poor thing begged like a dog hoping for a treat. Begging us to let him go so that he could see you again. Not that he would have actually *seen* you, given the circumstances, but I assumed he was speaking figuratively."

The cry of a raven echoes twice more.

"Why?" Rapunzel asks through tears of sorrow. "Why?"

Ruth laughs again. "I suppose that is the question, isn't it? Why? Why oh why did we slaughter your prince?"

Suddenly, the laughter stops, and Ruth's voice becomes cold, approaching sadistic. "I assure you, dear, it wasn't out of malice, anger, or even evil, as you probably believe. It was simply a matter of survival. You see, this forest has been cursed for a long time. And as the years go by, the sickness keeps spreading, slowly choking out all the life that remains in it, until there is nothing left." She snickers. "Why, I haven't seen so much as a single deer in these woods for years that was still alive after nightfall, much

less sheep or lambs. And out here in the middle of this forest, one tends to get hungry."

Devilish smile growing across her face, Ruth tilts her head, staring right into Rapunzel's eyes, watching as the terror begins to slowly creep in.

"After a while," the old woman continues, "I started to realize there was really only one source of food left. A harsh option, but one I much preferred to starving to death. Still, I'm not greedy. I don't take more than I need. Three is always enough to last the winter."

Thrice the raven cries in pain.

"Three is enough. No more, no less. But unfortunately, when dear old Rumple failed to deliver the third child, I was afraid we would starve to death out here during the long winter." Ruth's eyes suddenly light up. "Until I found your prince, wandering alone in the forest. A blind lamb, oblivious that it walked towards its own inevitable slaughter."

Dread turns to unimaginable disgust as the life leaves Rapunzel's soul.

"It's not often life gives us these little blessings," Ruth muses. "But when it does, you have to take advantage of it, seize the opportunity."

Tears stream down Rapunzel's face now as her head starts to twist, trying to deny it. Deny the horror.

"Consider this a blessing, child. Had I left him wandering in the woods, he'd have died anyway. At least this way you get to see him again."

Ruth offers a psychotic grin as she looks at the feast prepared on the table.

"You must admit, it's a beautiful spread."

Rapunzel tries to scream, but the cries get caught in her throat as she stares down in horror at the feast in which she herself has partaken, unable to look away, unable to run in terror.

Slowly, Ruth reaches down beneath the table and grabs the knife from Rapunzel's hands, flickers of evil growing along her face. "I'll be taking this, dear."

She sets the knife down upon the table, its silver glinting in the moonlight.

"I assume you were planning to kill me with it, should I discover the truth. Save you and your new friends from being cast out into the cold. A fine plan, I will admit. Unfortunately, for your sake, it was another false hope."

Ruth leans down, mere inches away from Rapunzel's horrified eyes.

"Now," she says, "I suppose you're wondering why you can't move."

Rapunzel tries to scream, tries to run, but all she can do is sit there, frozen, paralyzed, motionless, watching what takes place before her eyes.

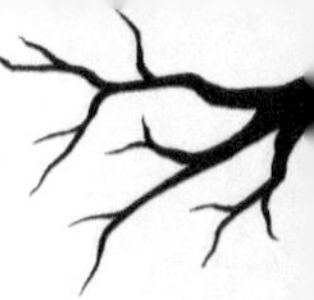

"It's simple, really," Ruth says, leaning back. "There is a plant that grows in this forest. It has… *unique* capabilities. Such as paralyzing you. I merely mixed it into your wine. But we'll get to that in a second."

With Rapunzel trapped at the dinner table, Ruth gets up from her seat and slowly walks over to the windowsill, grabbing a lantern that rests upon it.

"Did you know that in the olden times when a girl married a prince, they would anoint her head? A symbol of her becoming part of the kingdom, I suppose. A way of signifying her newfound royal blood, the changing of her stripes, as it were. When, of course, in reality, mere ointment cannot remove the stains of the past."

Ruth cracks the glass of the unlit lantern, letting the oil pour from it as she stands over Rapunzel, who is still unable to even scream for help.

"Nonetheless, given that you were about to marry a prince, I feel it is only right to extend you the same courtesy."

Desperately, Rapunzel tries to move, to scream, but she is forced to sit still, paralyzed, as Ruth removes her veil and tilts the lantern over her head, dripping oil all over her until it runs down her entire body.

When it's done, Ruth drops the lantern and moves back, taking a look at Rapunzel. "There we go. *Princess.*"

Then, as Rapunzel struggles to escape, Ruth slowly walks beside her, kneeling down and whispering into her ear.

"It's a strange feeling, isn't it? Not being able to move but knowing what's coming. I first tasted the plant when I was still a child. The townsfolk forced it down my throat, as well as my sister's. An old ritual, to keep witches from casting spells while they were burned alive."

Rapunzel's eyes cut down to Ruth's wrists, slightly revealed below her clothing.

Distorted skin. *Burned* skin.

"Do you know what it feels like, child?" Ruth asks as she stands back up and begins walking slowly towards the fireplace. "To be burned alive?"

"We have to go."

The stranger tries to pull Red toward the window, ready to break it and escape, even while she still shakes in terror.

Not yet willing to go, Red looks back to the door. "What about Rapunzel?"

The stranger closes his eyes before offering the solemn truth.

"It's too late for her."

Ruth steps closer to the fire.

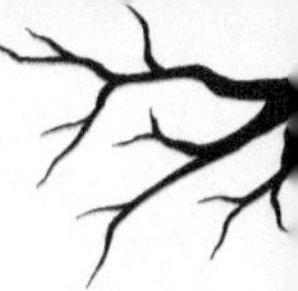

"First, you feel the heat," she says as flames reflect in her eyes. "For a moment, it's all you can feel as it spreads over you, a burning pain like nothing you've ever felt."

Finally, Rapunzel manages a squeal of terror as her body starts to shake in the chair, fear taking hold of her completely.

"Then, when you think the pain is over, it starts melting your skin. The fortunate ones have their eyes burned first, so they don't have to see themselves melt. But the unlucky ones…"

A maniacal laugh echoes throughout the cabin.

"We see *everything*."

The stranger breaks the bedroom window, shattering the glass and creating a single way to escape the monstrous presence within the cabin's walls.

As the storm rages outside, so fierce the rain blots the moon from view, the stranger reaches over, about to lead Red out into the forest when she hesitates once more.

"The knocking in the floor," she whispers as a look of newfound dread covers her face and her eyes drop down to the wood surface beneath the cot and the hidden door that lies within it. The one she hadn't noticed before, not until it was outlined in blood. The one with a single lock, trapping something inside.

"The basement," she whispers. "*Something's* down there."

"The fire…" Ruth says as she picks up a log from the fireplace and turns back, walking closer to Rapunzel. "The fire doesn't kill you quickly. No, it's a slow death. Agonizing. Every piece of your body being burned at once. Skin. Hair. Eyes. Everything in so much pain, the faint numbing of the body won't even set in."

She steps closer. The log in her hands leaves a trail of glowing embers falling down from it. A trail of burning ash leading straight to Rapunzel.

"Of course, the good news is, if you're paralyzed, you can't feel any of it. Not one bit."

An evil grin stretches across her wrinkled face.

"But you see, they didn't give me enough. The plant's effects wore off too quick, similar to how the effect is starting to wear off on you too. And while it might have allowed me to curse their wretched souls and escape, saving my sister in the process, it also meant I felt everything. Every burn, every second of anguish that lasted a lifetime as the fire burned my eyelids, forcing me to watch as it melted the skin from my body. As the fire reached my heart."

As Rapunzel struggles, she starts to move slightly, not enough to escape, but enough to feel again. Feel the heat of the fire growing closer.

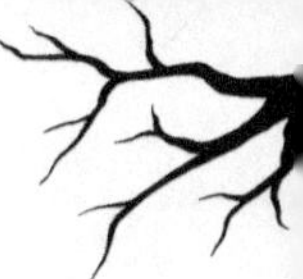

Ruth steps closer still, until finally she is standing right over Rapunzel, watching her struggle to scream as she bends down, and whispers quietly into her ear.

"You should have told me you just killed the witch. I could have forgiven that."

Ruth stands back tall, malicious glint in her eyes, burning log in her hands. Her head tilts slightly as she watches her victim struggling to escape.

"Oh, listen to me, prattling on about what it feels like to be burned alive."

She gives Rapunzel a final grin, holding the burning log above her.

"When I could just as easily show you."

Ruth drops it into Rapunzel's lap, laughing as she does, and its flames ignite the oil that drench the forsaken princess-to-be, in a mere breath causing her entire body to erupt in flames.

It's then that Rapunzel is finally able to scream.

The stranger opens the basement door.

As he does, the force breaks the lock like brittle oak.

The opening is small, and leads away from the room where they stand, away from the pair of bones hidden in the floorboards just behind them, towards a basement carved below the center of this cabin, a dark dungeon whose entrance is a hole of black, in a room unassuming, hiding victims unseen and cries unheard.

For a moment neither of them dares approach it, the pathway to more buried secrets hidden beneath the cabin's floor, as darkness seems to escape the hole, crawling up into the room, so thick they feel it in the air itself.

Cautious, Red inches closer towards it, somehow knowing what it contains. Hearing echoes of the torment in her head, the breaking of bones, the screaming of monsters, until finally she reaches it, holding her breath.

Standing over the basement, Red looks down at the victims trapped inside, curled up and shivering on the floor, revealed by the single light of a flickering flame. Two of them, a boy and a girl, barely ten years old.

The girl shakes in silence. The boy pleads with them, a single desperate request.

"Help us. Please."

PART SIX:
THE CHILDREN

CHAPTER TWENTY-FIVE

Near a great forest sits a small cottage home, fashioned from logs and resting upon a farm, one of the few sources of life left in the valley, for it is just out of the forest's reach.

Beside that cottage is a field, brightly lit by the morning sun, acres upon acres of dying land, withered wheat and

corrupted crops stretching out over the land only enough to cover the sullen soil that hid beneath.

Within that field are two small children playing in the grass, unaware of the twisted fate they will face before nightfall.

They run, they play, but finally they grow bored, as all children do, and so they look to the forest, at its twisting trees and tangled roots, daring to go where they know they shouldn't.

But they won't go far.

They never intended to go far.

"Slow down," Gretel says, panting as she runs through the trees, skipping over the rotten roots, unaware that they shift beneath her feet. "I can barely keep up."

Hansel looks back to his sister, cracking a sly grin but slowing down nonetheless.

Soon, they have ventured far beyond what they realized, progressing ever further into the forest's heart, looking in amazement at its tall trees and their jagged, winding branches.

For the children's hearts are too innocent to see the truth. The scars marked over every inch of the land, buried screams still trying to escape the dirt beneath, corpses torn apart, human and animal alike, with not enough left for even scavenging vultures to pick at.

"It's so beautiful here," Gretel says with wonder in her heart. "Nothing like the stories say."

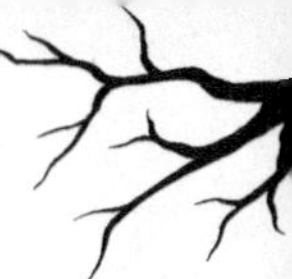

Hansel laughs. "That's because the stories are just fairy tales Mother tells us to keep us from playing in the woods."

At first Gretel giggles, but then she turns back to face the unending wilderness that seems to have already grown behind her, barely recognizing the stretch of land they wandered through only a moment ago.

As though the forest itself were changing.

"What if we get lost?" she asks.

"We won't. I promise." Hansel cracks a grin. "I'll make sure we can find our way out."

Gretel raises a curious eyebrow. "How?"

Hansel only winks, and they venture further still, the path to home, to safety, growing longer with every step, until the mere image of home becomes a far-off memory.

As they run, their laughter rings throughout the forest, echoing over the bones, above the dirt and between the trees, until finally, it reaches a cabin.

Then, a new kind of laughter echoes from within the cabin's walls.

Crazed, maniacal laughter.

Rain crashes down like a flood descending from oceans above as a storm appears out of nowhere, blocking the light from the sky and trapping everything in its suffocating grasp.

Including the children.

In the heart of the forest, trapped by the raging whirlwind, Hansel tries to lead his sister back home. Back the way they came.

But the storm is far too strong.

Both children fall to the ground, shaken by the wind and slipping in the mud, and as they lie there in the dirt, they begin to shiver from the freezing rain falling like sleet upon them. Their cold breath slowly rises from their bodies, twisting in the wind as if it were their ghosts abandoning their bodies to die in this evil place.

In reality, they are not so lucky.

In the light of day, they could have found their way home. Even in the darkness, they might have escaped. But in the storm, in rain so thick they can barely see their hands before their eyes, they'll never leave the forest alive.

Most probably, they won't leave it dead either.

The stories of this forest will come true.

But then, as everything around them seems to have grown dark, something flickers in the distance. A single light within the forest, a single ember all alone against the black grip of death, and yet it remains, signaling life. Signaling hope.

As the girl in red will do soon enough, and as so many have done before, they believed the beautiful lie of hope.

"There, a light." Hansel points to it, hopeful. "Light means fire."

Gretel nods, standing up from the mud beside him. "Fire means warmth."

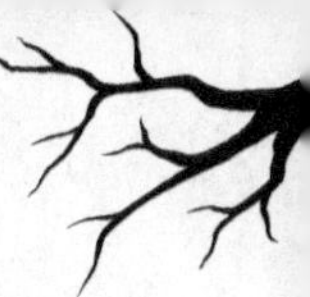

Then, in a moment they will come to regret for the rest of their lives, they run towards the light.

"Help us!" Hansel screams.

They run through the forest as fast as they can, rain crashing down against them, thunder trying to drown out their desperate cries for help.

"Help!"

Finally, they reach a clearing within the trees. Thin traces of moonlight push through the storm clouds above, revealing the cabin in front of them, and the small fire burning within it.

"Help!" Gretel screams.

Their misguided prayers are answered as the cabin door suddenly opens and an old woman steps outside, the outline of her features traced by the fire burning in the fireplace behind her.

When she sees the children, she stretches out her arms and calls out in a kind, gentle tone. "Come here, out of the storm."

Behind them, a raven cries out, a desperate cry of warning that goes unheeded as the children run to the cabin, unaware of the monster that waits within.

All while the raven can only watch.

More children stolen in the night…

CHAPTER TWENTY-SIX

esting on the soft couch, wrapped in warm blankets, the children lie shielded from the storm by the cabin's creaking walls.

On the old chair in front of them, Ruth sits, drinking warm tea from a cup of chipped porcelain, eyeing them over curiously.

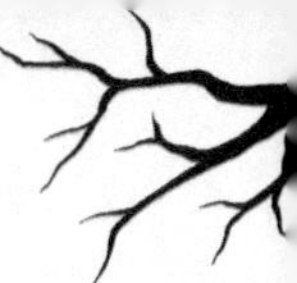

"What are two young children like yourselves doing out here in these woods all by your lonesomes?" Ruth asks between sips of tea. "You're probably giving your mother a heart attack."

Gretel speaks first, savoring every moment of warmth within the blanket, the chill of the forest still on her skin. "We were just playing when the storm came. We didn't mean to get lost, I promise."

"Children never mean to get lost, dear." Ruth grins. "But it happens all the same."

As her words hang in the air, a moment of uncomfortable silence lingers, until finally Hansel speaks. "Thank you for saving us."

"Oh, I would hardly call it saving you. I simply couldn't turn away two children in need of help. Anyone would do the same."

"Still," Gretel says, gratitude in her voice. "Thank you."

Ruth grins once more. "Oh, you are most welcome, dear."

As the storm rages outside, the helpless guests begin to enjoy the comfort of the cabin, unaware of the witch that drinks tea before their eyes.

"Are you alone in this cabin?" Hansel asks.

Ruth looks to her kitchen, seeing the barren cabinets, the empty table. "Yes," she answers. "I'm alone. Although, I do have an old friend who's coming to visit soon."

Cracking a sly grin, she turns her eyes to the children. "Rumor has it he's bringing me a present from the kingdom up north."

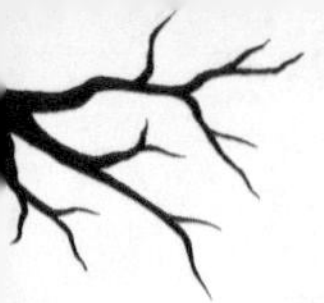

Fascinated at the mention of the kingdom, the children lean forward with interest.

"What is it?" Gretel asks with the curious mind of a child.

"Oh, it's nothing much," Ruth says, waving her hand to dismiss it. "Just something to help survive the winter."

Lightning flashes.

A raven cries out at the top of its lungs, diving down through the rain and crashing into the cabin's window. The children recoil in shock, too afraid of the dark bird to hear its even darker warning.

Finally, the raven flies away, leaving a hairline crack in the window as a reminder of the children it tried to save. The children who wandered willingly into death's own cabin.

Once Gretel regains her breath from the shock of the raven, she begins to look around the cabin in amazement. Before long, Hansel does as well.

Ruth smiles gently. "Do you want to hear a secret, children?"

They nod their heads, and Ruth leans in closer, whispering the words to them as if she were a kind grandmother.

"This cabin has magic within it. It can appear as the thing you want most in this world." She watches as their eyes light up with excitement. "Tell me, children, what do you see when you look at its walls?"

Reflections of magic bloom in her eyes as Gretel smiles in amazement. "I see… candy."

"I do too," Hansel says, eyes widened.

For a moment, all they can do is look at its walls, its furniture, hearts full of wonder as they see delicious candy within every inch.

In their wonder, they don't see the way Ruth is looking at them. The desperation behind her eyes.

"If you truly see a house made of candy," Ruth says, "then you both must be very hungry children."

In a single breath their excitement fades, and they both look down, suddenly embarrassed.

Slowly, Ruth walks over and pats their shoulders. "There is no reason to be ashamed of hunger, children. Everyone within reach of this forest feels the same. The land was cursed long ago."

Her eyes glance to the barren kitchen once more, remembering a lifetime of hunger, of starvation-fueled agony.

"Now," she continues, "we all just do what we have to in order to survive. To eat, to feast. Why, I bet your mother is home right now, preparing a dinner for when you return."

She speaks the words gently, holding her breath for a response that the girl is innocent enough to give.

"Our mother isn't home right now."

Ruth hides the evil grin growing across her face. "What? Why ever not?"

"Our parents," Hansel says, "they left for the kingdom, searching for food. They said once they returned, we wouldn't have to go hungry anymore."

Ruth's head begins to tilt as the grin becomes too large to hide. "Your father is gone too? They left you all alone?"

"Not all of us could make the trip," Gretel says, "and it's only a week's journey. We can care for ourselves until then with what food is left."

"A week's journey?" Ruth cackles slightly, almost imperceptibly. "No, no, no, that won't do. I can't just leave two children alone out here, especially in these woods. Who knows what could happen? You can stay here until they return."

"Oh," Hansel says, "we don't want to trouble you. Really, we will be okay by ourselves."

"Nonsense," Ruth says, waving her hand. "You'll stay here, where it's safe."

Lightning strikes, and thunder shakes the cabin, causing the chill of dread to crawl over Gretel's skin as she imagines being back out there in the storm.

"Thank you," she says, grateful for the shelter offered.

"Of course, dear," Ruth says. "Now…"

Her eyes spark madness.

"Let me show you to your room."

CHAPTER TWENTY-SEVEN

As the children walk into the small bedroom, still illuminated by the glowing light of the fire's embers, Ruth gently guides them towards the bed, the small cot on which they foolishly believe they will spend the night, lying on its comfort.

At this point, however, even if they had known the truth, they have ventured too far into the monster's lair, and it would do them no good to scream, for they would be calling out to no one, and it would do them no good to run, for it would only delay the inevitable.

So, for a few more precious moments of innocence, they approach the cot, looking around the small bedroom, magic still in their eyes.

"I do have one further question," Ruth says. "If you will permit an old woman's curiosity."

"Of course," Gretel answers with a smile.

"Why would you come into these woods?" Ruth asks, her tone shifting ever so slightly, becoming haunting, almost hideous. "Surely you've heard the stories told. Of the monster who lives here, listening for the laughter of children."

Her grip on their shoulders tightens as worry begins to creep onto their faces, and her tone grows darker still.

"The stories of the children who come into these woods, never to return. Who vanish from the world outside, never to be seen again."

Ruth's bony fingers dig into the children's skin as they try to move away, while she just stares off into nothing.

"Never to escape the forest alive."

Finally, squealing in pain, Gretel speaks up. "You're hurting us."

A sudden look of realization passes over Ruth, and she immediately releases her grip on their shoulders.

"Forgive me, my dear," she pleads, offering a smile.

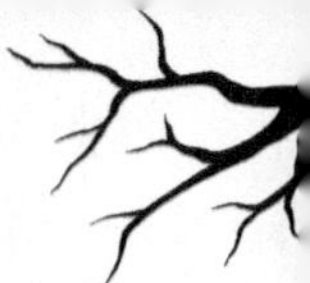

Silence echoes, as the children begin to feel it. What they should have felt all along. The aura of death surrounding them, filling the air, crawling into their bones. The horrible secret within this cabin.

With a hint of fear in his voice, Hansel asks a question that he now dreads the answer to. "Is… this our room?"

Ruth cackles. "No, of course not, child…"

Her grip on their shoulders returns. But this time, it is gentle. Almost motherly, ushering them back into a false sense of calm once more.

"You'll be staying beneath the floor."

"What?" Gretel asks, nervous voice cracking.

Ruth notices the rising anxiety hidden in the child's words and attempts to feign innocence by walking over to the cot and lifting it up, revealing the door hidden beneath it.

"There is a basement to this cabin," she says. "It is where you both can stay."

Slowly, Ruth lifts up the door and motions her head to the small opening beneath it, revealing stairs that lead only into darkness.

"Well…" She grins. "Don't be shy. Have a closer look."

Gretel almost takes a step closer, if only out of nervousness, but Hansel takes her hand, pulling her back, terror erupting in his eyes.

"Th-thank you," he stutters. "But… I think we should leave."

Slowly, the children begin to walk backwards.

Ruth tilts her head, still holding up the charade of kindness. "But you only just got here, and the storm still rages outside. Why don't you rest for the night, and you can return home in the morning?"

Still, they move back, almost reaching the door as Hansel nervously speaks. "No, thank you."

In a single instant, insanity and rage spread over Ruth, turning her into something unrecognizable as she motions towards the door and makes a final harsh request with a biting tongue.

"Get in."

They back away. "No."

Then, to their surprise, Ruth laughs. Loudly, maniacally, like a crazed lunatic torturing a defenseless animal. And when she speaks, it is as though death speaks through her.

"So be it."

From the storm is born lightning, and the door behind them shuts itself, trapping them in the room, defenseless against the witch.

She grabs Gretel first.

The child screams as she is dragged towards the hole in the floor that leads to the basement. Leads to darkness.

"No!" Gretel screams. "Please!"

Hansel tries to fight, to save his sister, but Ruth shoves him aside like a rag doll before looking to Gretel once more,

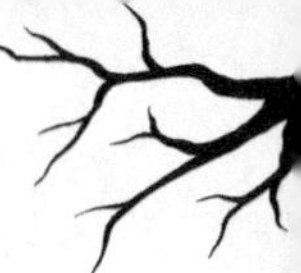

holding her above the foul basement's entrance, savoring how the child squeals for her life.

"Please!" Gretel begs through tears.

Ruth only cackles. "You shouldn't have come into my forest."

In an instant, the witch releases her grip, and Gretel drops down, falling into the hole, vanishing within a darkness so all-consuming it is as though she no longer existed.

The only trace of her left is the sound of her frail body crashing into the ground below.

"No!" Hansel screams as he stands up from the floor and runs to the basement door, looking down into its depths, hoping to see his sister, still alive.

Ruth circles him from behind.

"Don't worry, child," she says. "I won't kill you immediately. I'll wait until winter arrives, until your parents have given up searching for you. Until the hunger sets in."

Laughing, she kicks Hansel down, watching him vanish from sight in the darkness. Then she closes the door, trapping them both beneath the floor, cackling as she hears them cry.

"Children," Ruth laughs. "They always cry."

CHAPTER TWENTY-EIGHT

In the dark, hidden away beneath the earth within the confines of the cabin, trapped within its soil as though they were corpses buried long ago, the children sit quietly, crying to themselves.

The darkness is all-consuming, revealing not even their own bodies, nothing except the festering blackness of death,

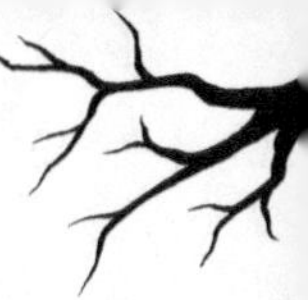

yet they can still feel what is down there with them, what surrounds them even now.

Bones. The skeletons of previous children. Those who wandered into the forest just as they did, never to be heard from again, trapped beneath this cabin even in death.

As her hand brushes against one and she feels the echoes of stolen life still crawling within the cracks of its skull, Gretel begins to weep once more, and Hansel moves to her, holding her in his arms, trying not to cry.

Trying to be strong for his sister.

Days pass, feeling like years spent trapped within the cabin's graveyard, among the ghosts of previous victims, hearing nothing but silence, until…

A sound echoes above them. The voice of a man, calling out for help.

Gretel starts to scream in return, but Hansel covers her mouth, whispering to her softly.

"She'll hear us."

Slowly, he removes his hand, and they both stay quiet, listening as the man's footsteps echo above them, joined by those of the witch, and her old friend who's come to visit.

As he listens to the footsteps, Hansel gets an idea. The only way to cry out for help without the witch noticing.

That night, the children beat against the walls of the basement, trying to cry out, hoping the witch will think it's just the house creaking in the wind, but praying the man will find out the truth.

Desperate, they continue to beat against the wall until their hands bleed, their crimson the only color visible in a room of stolen light as tears fall from their faces.

Within the bloodstained walls, they cry out.

But it's no use.

For walls of dirt make no echo.

Defeated, they collapse back to the ground, Hansel's hands still hitting the bloodstained wall in desperation, but he knows it's over. Their cries would alert the witch, the walls make no sound, and there is nothing else in the room with which to make an echo. There's nothing else in the room at all, save for blood, and...

All at once, Hansel shudders, seeing the horrible salvation.

Skeletons. Bones. Skulls.

The only tools left to make a sound.

With a reluctant hand, Hansel lifts a skull up, and crashes it back down against another, making a sharp crack, like a crack of lightning or the creaking of wood. Knowing they have no other choice, soon Gretel joins in, until at last the sound echoes above them, rising from the basement, up through the floorboards, before ringing out in the bedroom of the blind prince, who is awoken from his slumber.

Confused and even more concerned, the prince listens closely, hearing the knocking within the floor, and a chill crawls down his spine as he hears it echoing from beneath him the entire night.

But he does not understand what it means, for he is trapped in darkness the same as them, only his darkness could not be removed by the sun, for it has been stolen from him forever.

Another night falls, and again, the children beat against the walls and crash skulls together, hoping the man will hear them and come to their rescue, as if it were the ending to one of the storybooks their mother reads them so often.

That dream born of delusion fades as they hear the footsteps, the screaming, the struggle above them, until finally they see the bright red creeping down from the cracks, and as the blood rains down upon them, they realize the prince needed saving of his own.

More days pass, until the memory of light is but a harsh shadow in the children's mind, until they dare not hope for escape, lest the suffering become ever crueler.

It is then that they hear another voice.

The voice of a girl, crying out for help, afraid of a monster lurking in the forest.

As the children hear it, hope doesn't even flicker in their eyes. The thought of escape is a distant memory, a beautiful lie designed to crush their souls.

No, they don't dream of escape.

They dream of warning the girl. Of sparing her from the same fate.

That night, the children cry out with crashing skulls louder than before, desperately trying to warn the girl. Warn her of what the old woman is, of the victims that lie hidden beneath the floor among them, praying she'll hear their message and escape the witch's grasp under the veil of secret night.

Had the girl lain in the bed above them, she might have heard it clearly. Instead, she lies in the room across from them, just close enough to hear their knocking, but much too far away to know the truth behind the sounds. The knocking's true origin.

Someone else, however, does heed the message.

A shadow, created by the raging fire within the fireplace, moves closer to the basement door.

Thin, wrinkled fingers reach down, ripping the door open, looming over the children, who look up in fear.

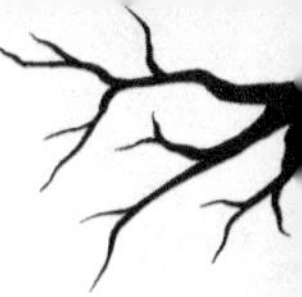

The monster above them holds a lantern and begins to descend the steep steps, watching as the children become silent as mice at her mere presence.

"Did you think I wouldn't hear it?" Ruth asks, her twisted shadow flickering over the children as if it were her true form, fire revealing the melted flesh that a dozen spells could barely hide. "Did you think me too old to notice?"

Step by step, she descends, restrained anger in her voice.

"What did you think would happen?" she asks. "Did you think the girl could save you?"

Step by step, she draws closer to them, psychotic features illuminated by the lantern's fire.

"No one can save you," she whispers. "Not from me. I will not die in this forest. I will not allow myself to starve."

She reaches the final step, the bottom of the basement, freezing for a moment as she does.

"I'll kill you first."

In a sudden flash of movement, she drops the lantern, causing a loud crash to echo through the house as the witch moves to Hansel, clasping her wrinkled hands around his throat, backing him against the wall.

As the lantern flickers, she whispers to him.

"If I hear another sound from below the floorboards… a single knock of bones, a single cry for help… if I even hear the cabin itself creak, I won't come back down here. At least, not at first."

Ruth leans in closer.

"But when I do come back down, when I do eventually come for you, if I've heard a single peep from within the floor, I will throw your sister into the furnace first, and make you watch as I roast her like a lamb."

A tear falls down Hansel's cheek. Gretel sobs beside him.

"Do you understand me, boy?" Ruth snarls. "You will watch her burn."

Hansel cries in terror but manages to nod.

In a single breath, Ruth's cruel, sinister expression turns back into one of kindness.

"Good," she exclaims. "I'm glad we have an understanding."

As she turns to walk away, she leaves the lantern on the floor beside them, ascending back up the steps. But before she closes the basement door, she whispers a final warning.

"Not. A. Sound."

The door closes.

In the flickering light of the lantern, surrounded by illuminated skeletons of past children, so many they dare not count, Hansel and Gretel cry alone.

Cry in silence.

CHAPTER TWENTY-NINE

The next day, as the children still weep in silence, afraid to even breathe lest the witch should hear them, more noises begin to echo from the cabin, voices that paint a portrait of the events happening above in the light.

Another man's voice, this one darker.

Then a woman, calling out.

All the while, Hansel and Gretel sit in silence, not daring to even move.

The strangers above enter the cabin. A conversation ensues. Harsh words and biting tongues echoing above them, along with tales of torment, of lost princes and chasing monsters.

Later, they hear the muffled sounds of bloodshed as the young woman above them slaughters the old man.

Then the children hear the cracking of floorboards as something is hidden within the floor of the room where the prince was slain, where his blood rained down, the same room that contained the door that led to the basement where they had fallen. If they'd ripped up the floorboards only a few feet over, those above might've found those below. But instead of saving the souls of those trapped in darkness, instead another victim is added to them. Hidden within the dirt that lies below the house. Another skeleton for its collection.

So close to salvation, and yet it wasn't to be.

At least, not yet.

They hear the dinner, then the screaming, and finally, they hear the fire raging above them, mixing with the screams of the young woman who called out from the forest.

Shedding tears of mourning in silence, the children think it's over. Thinking the witch has slaughtered them all. But then, the unthinkable happens.

The basement door opens.

Above them stands a young girl in a red hood. Beside her stands a stranger.

Gretel shakes, still too afraid to speak, but Hansel finds the strength to plead one final request of life, one last desperate attempt at hope.

"Help us. Please."

PART SEVEN:
THE WITCH

CHAPTER THIRTY

Red stares down at the stolen children, far too afraid and much too shocked to move as everything around her seems to grow still. Even the cracks of lightning and the falling of rain take a reprieve from their violent storm. In the distance, a raven can be heard, a single cry stretching out for an eternity, as though it were echoing slowly across a forest within her mind, as she witnesses the true secrets buried underneath the innocent cabin.

Illuminated by a single lantern, softly burning on the basement floor, the children appear thin, far thinner than they should be. The result of more than a week trapped beneath the living, fed only the occasional crumbs that the witch allowed to fall through the cracked floorboards above their heads.

Tears form in their eyes as the boy pleads once more. "Help us."

The words hang in the air, softly repeating in Red's thoughts as she hears her own voice. All the times she wished for help that never came, the times she heard the footsteps coming for her, when she'd plead with the empty night itself to save her, knowing it never would.

Finally, memories of the past shock her into action, and she stretches out her hand, an offering of help, of salvation from the depths of madness where they lie trapped. Accepting it, the boy moves up the stairs, taking Red's hand, allowing her to lead him out of the basement, the coffin of earth his still-breathing corpse was placed in, and back into the light, into the cabin, where rain beats against the walls once more and thunder shakes the very floor.

To most, signs of horror. To the boy, signs of comfort, for they are proof that he is back among the living, proof that light still exists.

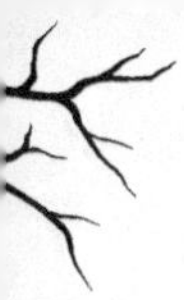
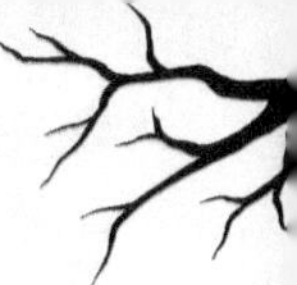

But the girl will not go.

Too terrified to move, Gretel merely shivers where she stands, not willing to escape the basement. Not willing to hope, lest the monster should catch her.

As Red looks down at the girl, barely ten years old and already afraid of the world and the monsters within it, a memory flashes in her head, and she no longer sees the girl.

She sees herself.

Crying alone underneath her bed, wrapped in a crimson hood, wishing that she could vanish within it forever, wanting desperately to run away from her home, from her torment, from her own private monsters.

But fear kept her there for years.

As she watches herself for a final moment, her younger reflection looks to her, begging her without words to save her from this nightmare. And as the memory fades and Red sees the girl once more, she recognizes the same look in her eyes.

Begging for help that she no longer believes will come.

A single tear falls down Red's face, and the emotions gripping her heart, the fear, the pain, the loss, they change, shift and grow like the forest outside, until all that's left is quiet resolve as she descends the steps, entering the basement hidden beneath the floor. Entering into the nightmare she once escaped.

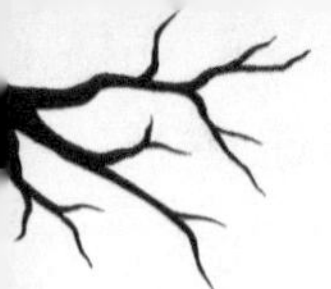

The wood creaks with every step as she descends further, causing the children above and below to flinch alike, afraid of alerting the witch.

But fear does not crawl its way into Red's heart. Not anymore.

Instead, she reaches out her hand, brushing away the young girl's tears.

As the girl looks up into Red's eyes, not a word is spoken, and yet, she understands. The girl before her knows it all. All the things she is too scared to say, all the shame caused by that which they couldn't control yet blamed themselves for anyway. But she also sees something else.

The need to run. The will to fight.

Most of all, she sees a friend ready to help, a sign that she is not alone and never will be again.

Finally, Red holds out her hand, and Gretel takes it, allowing herself to be led up from the basement that has become the tomb of so many others, whose fragile skeletons still rest below within its confines of death.

As they ascend, the fire goes with them, shining brightly from the lantern, which Red now holds up with her spare hand, guiding their ascension like a phoenix rising from the ashes of a burning forest whose fire was never extinguished.

With each step, Red remembers who she once was.

The scared girl she will never be again.

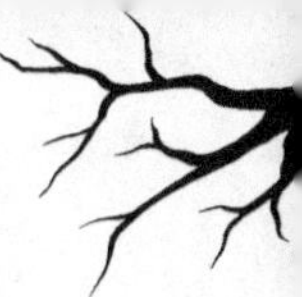

A final step is taken, and they reach the bedroom once more, both children embracing for a moment as Red and the stranger look back down at the basement, now shrouded in darkness once more.

In each other's eyes, they find echoes of an idea and share a silent nod of agreement as Red holds the lantern over the dark pit of hidden bodies and stolen children. It burns just as it did when it sat in the cabin's window, signaling hope to those searching for it. Luring them to this wretched place.

Now, it will be the very thing that destroys it.

With resolve in her heart, Red drops the lantern.

Fire eats away at the darkness as the flame falls, slowly revealing the skeletons of the children once more, bathing them in an orange hue of burning flames growing ever closer, until finally the lantern hits the ground and its glass shatters, allowing the fire to escape.

Slowly, like a bloodied animal limping from a snare, the fire crawls out of the lantern, finally taking hold of the ground and spreading across it, until in a sudden raging flash the entire basement erupts in flames.

As the fire reaches up, scattered embers escaping the secret door that once led to darkness, Red now shuts it to blot out the burning light.

Closing the basement door forever.

CHAPTER THIRTY-ONE

In the middle of a great forest lies a cabin. Within the cabin lies a kitchen. Within that kitchen lies a large wooden dining table where a witch now sits, quietly enjoying her meal, savoring the silence while it lasts.

A flash of silver glints as Ruth cuts a piece of meat, using the knife stolen from Rapunzel to carve her dinner.

Slowly, she raises it up to her mouth, taking a bite, enjoying the pleasant flavor before finally looking over to Rapunzel, whose charred remains still sit upright in the chair but whose screams have long gone silent.

For a moment longer, Ruth stares at the corpse, remembering her own skin, what she once looked like after the flames, as though she were looking in a mirror. Only this time, her mind isn't broken from pain or distorted with growing madness.

For she went mad long ago.

Suddenly, her quiet reflection is broken by the sound of the basement door slamming shut, and she grins, cutting her eyes to the bedroom.

"Why do they always run?"

Covered in a hood of shimmering crimson, trapped within a small bedroom with a monster of ill intent lurking right outside, Red holds Gretel's hand tightly and points to the window, asking without words.

The stranger nods.

Tragic events of the night having long since driven the memories of what chased her in the forest from her

recollection, Red moves to the window, ready to break it and escape the witch's lair.

But it appears fate is far too cruel to allow that.

Lightning strikes in the sky, and scattered shards of splintered wood burst in the air. A moment later, the lightning's victim is revealed as a broken tree falls down atop the cabin, its thick, twisting branches pushing their way through the now-shattered window.

Trapping the cabin's guests inside.

The children cry.

Red turns to the stranger. "What do we do?"

Silence lingers for a breath before finally he sighs, resigned to the tragedy.

"We have to go through the house."

At his words, the children cry louder, not wanting to face the witch for fear they shall never escape her sight again.

But as they move closer to the bedroom door, Red attempts to calm them, whispering softly in their ears. "When we open the door, I need you to run. Okay?" She tries to force her voice to be strong, knowing that if they don't run, they'll never escape. "She won't catch us if we run."

"Promise?" Gretel asks through tears.

Red denies her own fright and looks into the girl's eyes, making a vow that she prays she can keep. "Promise."

A second later, they open the door, ready to run.

But Ruth waits just on the other side, standing in the doorway, head tilted, grin stretched across her face.

They jump back in terror.

The witch merely chuckles, focusing her eyes on Red. "Are you okay, dear? You look a little pale."

Hands shaking, Red moves back further, eyes going bloodshot as she waits to see what Ruth will do.

In return, Ruth takes a single step forward, and again, they shift backwards.

"My my," Ruth cackles. "Aren't you jumpy. Is something the matter?"

Her gaze turns to the stranger, still ignoring the children as if they weren't even there, and in the witch's eyes Red sees a test, a curiosity about what the stranger will do, if he will cower in fear like the rest.

The witch receives her answer as the stranger meets her gaze, unwilling to cower to her, and as Red sees his hands, sees his eyes, she notices that for the first time since he arrived at the cabin, they don't flinch, don't shake. Instead, they appear calm. Hauntingly so. As though for the first time since coming here, his bones and flesh were in agreement on what needed to be done.

Whatever that is, Red isn't sure she wants to know.

The witch returns a curious look, but finally her attention turns to the children, even as she still speaks to Red.

"I see you found my other guests. Why don't you bring them out to dinner? I'm sure our dear Rapunzel has been *dying* for some company."

With the invitation spoken, she turns and slowly walks out of the bedroom.

The rest of them stand motionless, dread crawling over their skin like spiders, until finally they follow, knowing they have no other choice.

Footsteps softly echo from them as they move out from the door into the narrow hallway where the cabin seems to be growing smaller, and finally to the kitchen, where the footsteps stop, and they see Ruth standing beside the dining table, next to the charred corpse of Rapunzel.

The children scream.

Red cries.

Ruth smiles. "She did have such beautiful hair."

The smile turns to a chuckle, the chuckle to a cackle, and the cackle into psychotic, maniacal laughter, all the while tears stream down Red's face as she mourns for her friend.

As the witch laughs and the storm outside rages ever fiercer, the stranger speaks to Red, never taking his eyes off Ruth.

"Take the children," he tells her. "Go. Now."

In her mourning, Red looks to him with confusion, not yet willing to lose another friend. "What about you?"

"Just go," he pleads.

Her eyes water with sorrow at the sacrifice, knowing he'll die, yet would stay anyway. A life laid down just to give them time, a chance to escape with their lives.

In all her years of torment, no one has ever helped her.

Red looks to the stranger, giving him a final nod of indescribable gratitude that he meets in turn, before taking the children's hands and running out of the door, not daring to look back at the cackling witch.

They run from the house, feet digging into the mud, skin pierced by the rain crashing down from above them as they venture into the forest's heart.

Within mere moments, they vanish from sight within the trees.

CHAPTER THIRTY-TWO

With no children to scare and no girl in red to frighten, Ruth stops laughing and cuts her eyes to the stranger, evil intentions flickering within them. Not caring to meet her gaze, the stranger only looks out the window, praying Red can escape the forest before

222

the monster catches her, eyes lifted up at the storm clouds blotting out the night sky, not even allowing a single trace of moonlight to shine through.

Slowly, he turns back to the witch.

At first, not a word is spoken as they silently face off against one another, one of them a monstrous witch whose true nature has been revealed, the other only a stranger whose past is not yet known.

"I'll catch them, you know," Ruth says. "Your death won't so much as delay that, sickeningly noble as it may be."

The stranger says nothing.

"I'll hunt them down," she continues, slowly walking around the dinner table, passing by the cursed food and the charred princess. "The children I'll save, of course, but Red… no, no, no. She'll die slow. I'll slaughter her in the forest and leave her carcass there to *rot*."

Still, the stranger says nothing.

"I am curious, though," the witch says, stopping in front of a candle, letting its light reveal her in a hue of orange flames, appearing as though she were burning even now. "How did you know it was not lamb?"

The only response is that of a raven crying out in the distance, for of all the creatures in this forest, it's the only one who knows the true nature of every beast, who sees all from its perch high in the twisting branches, forever forced to watch helplessly as the tragic tale unfolds beneath it.

All it can do is cry out in warning.

With no answer to her inquiry, Ruth sighs, moving still further across the table, lifting up the knife of silver. "Very well, then. You shall die a mystery."

Lightning strikes, and the witch vanishes from sight.

The stranger backs up, turning his head to and fro in shock, searching for where the witch has gone. But although her body has vanished, her voice remains, echoing throughout the house.

"I am this cabin, boy. I am its walls, its wood, its very soul."

The stranger turns once more as darkness begins to literally crawl across the cabin until it envelops it completely, choking out every last trace of light, leaving only the absence of a void. Eternal blackness.

"You don't know what horror is. What a curse can do."

In the dark, something cuts the stranger across his back, drawing crimson blood, the only color visible in the pitch-black room.

"I could cast a spell, forcing you to go blind, as the other witch did to the poor, innocent prince."

Another flash of silver, and more blood pours from the stranger's stomach.

"Or I could curse you as I cursed the young woman years ago. Turn you into a bird, a raven, a filthy animal who eats worms from the dirt."

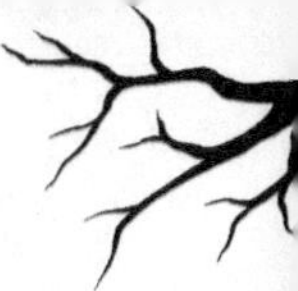

Ravens begin to appear, crawling out from the ground, horribly deformed and calling out for help.

The stranger tries to run, but a silver knife pushes into his side, slipping between his ribs. A second later, it disappears once more, leaving only the dripping red blood as a sign on the wound.

"Or perhaps I could curse your mind. Force you to run into the forest and find Red for me. Drag her back here and kill her yourself."

The darkness begins to crawl up the stranger's leg, slowly covering him, until he too vanishes within the room of shadows, as though he didn't exist anymore. For in the darkness, the only sign of life is a scream, but no call for help echoes from him, nor does a cry of pain.

"But then again, you're far too pathetic to waste a good spell on. Because behind all your mystery, all your lies, I know who you are, stranger."

In an instant, the darkness fades and the cabin reappears, as does Ruth, who shoves the stranger over, holding him against the dinner table with her thin, bony fingers and whispering into his ear.

"You're *nothing*."

As lightning flashes outside, the witch lifts up the knife and stabs him in the heart.

"You have no story in this forest. No role to play in this tale."

Removing the knife while the biting words still echo, spilling his blood on the table beneath him, Ruth watches the crimson crawling across the feast until the food finally resembles the horror it truly is. Then, with the carelessness one might use to discard a rotten piece of meat, Ruth opens the door and pushes him out of it, watching as his dying body collides with the cold ground.

Still alive, but not for long.

Yet, on the ground, as he looks up to see her slowly walking out of the cabin towards her prey, he sees what she does not. A bright reflection in his eyes. The fire, slowly escaping the confines of the basement. Slowly growing out of control.

Soon, it will spread to the cabin itself, where even the rain cannot stop it.

Oblivious to the fire, Ruth looms over him, bloodied knife in her hands. But still she doesn't stab him, doesn't finish her prey, end his suffering. Instead, she leans down, whispering to him once more.

"You'll die where we found you. In the *dirt*."

Then, as the stranger's eyes go white, as his pierced heart gives out and he breathes his last, Ruth stands back up, turning her attention to the forest and the trail of muddied footprints Red left behind.

She shakes her head in disappointment.

"Why do they always run?"

CHAPTER THIRTY-THREE

Clouds above hide the sky, replacing it with erratic cracks of lightning and booming thunder echoing across the land as the girl in red runs through the forest.

Fighting against the wind and the rain, trying to escape not only for herself but for the children whose fate

mirrors her own past, who now run beside her, slipping in the mud, holding tight to her hands for support.

Above them, a raven follows, beating its wings hard in the air, struggling against the torrent just to stay in the sky.

Through the dark, endless expanse of twisting branches and rotting roots, streaks of crimson flash as a red hood moves swiftly between the trees, sparks of bright color appearing for a moment, then vanishing back behind the trees, over and over again.

After what feels like a lifetime, hope finally grows on Red's face, and for only a moment, she thinks they can actually escape the monster.

But then the witch's voice echoes around them.

"You think you can run?"

The shock of hearing evil's true voice causes Red to stumble, but she doesn't stop running. Fear won't let her.

"You think you can escape this forest? That anyone can?"

Suddenly, the forest surrounding Red seems to move, the branches themselves reaching out to take hold of her, to steal away the children.

"This forest belongs to me, as does everything that enters it. It does what I command. Its own branches move as I wish them to."

As they run, the branches stretch farther, breaking themselves as they try to grab hold of Red, trying to trap her in their grasp. But as they do, Red sees the splinters

of bark falling from them, and she realizes something for the first time.

The forest is not evil.

It never was.

Its trees are trapped here the same as her, forced to mutilate themselves at Ruth's command, slaves of a witch trying to trap the only souls that give the forest life. The chill on her bones, the feeling of death that cascades over everything that enters within, it isn't the trees calling out for their prey, more victims to rot in their dirt. It is the moaning of agony, the very soil growing so soulless, scarring itself so deep, that nothing dares enter in, to save those whom it would be forced to slaughter by an evil presence.

The forest is a victim, the same as her.

Still, she has to escape it, and as courage courses through her body, she manages to push through the branches, to break free from those that wrap themselves around her arms.

The children, however, are not so lucky.

A jagged branch takes hold of Gretel's ankle, pulling her down into the dirt, tearing away at her skin. Desperately, Red picks her back up, trying to pull her through the forest even as Hansel is tripped by another branch, grasping its withered bark around his frail arm.

"Perhaps you can escape," the witch's voice rings out, *"if you leave them behind."*

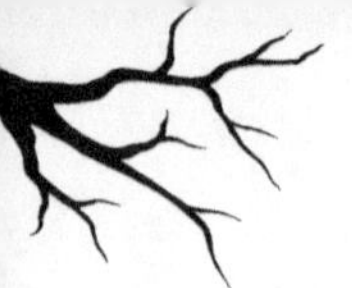

Red pulls against the branches, trying to break the children free.

"I promise I'll take good care of them for you."

Finally, Red frees them, and they run once more, her crimson hood now torn as it flows behind her. And as they try to escape, memories flash in Red's mind. Memories of running through this forest before.

Memories of a monster chasing her.

Suddenly, her gaze cuts down to Gretel's ankle, and upon witnessing the blood drawn by the branch, her eyes echo a fresh thought that becomes a horrific reminder. The ankle is cut, but that's all it is. All jagged wood can do. But her own wound, the still-stinging gash carved into her leg, it's different. It's not a mere cut but a piece of flesh torn open.

Something a branch could not do.

Red shivers. *Something else is in these woods.*

Suddenly, something catches their feet, and they stumble in the mud, passing through haunting trees.

As her body hits the ground and she grunts in pain, her desperate gaze is forced upwards to the clouds above, seeing no trees, no branches to block her view, no sign of the forest. For a moment, a rush of emotion floods over her.

Hope.

They made it out…

But then, as she starts to stand, dizzy from the fall and rain pouring down over her, she sees the truth. They haven't escaped. They've merely stumbled into a field, a large clearing within the trees.

A clearing covered with… *Oh no, it's not… it's not possible…*

Not this many… not in one place… it's not… not…

Gretel screams. Hansel follows.

The breath of life within her is stolen as Red sees what frightened the children. That which would frighten even the darkest of monsters.

The clearing. It's covered in bones.

Human bones.

Hundreds of them, scattered in the dirt, rotting away with decay, along with remnants of broken wood where houses must once have been.

A town that lived within the forest.

A village slaughtered long ago.

Laughter soon echoes from within the trees as Ruth slowly steps out from them.

"You know, I was actually going to let you live."

As she steps into the clearing, into the vast graveyard that lies above the soil, the trees behind her seem to bend closer, bark shifting and branches breaking.

"I've never let anyone live. Not once. But I felt sorry for you. I was going to show you kindness."

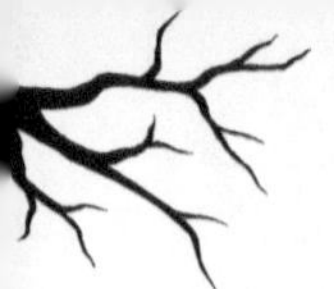

Lightning flashes over and over before thunder can even echo.

"And you repay me by stealing what's mine?" the witch snarls. "By leaving me to starve alone out in the forest?"

She steps closer to Red, the psychotic grin leaving her face for a moment, appearing kind for the last time.

"Maybe we can still part ways as friends. Maybe if you leave the children, I'll let you escape with your life."

Red trembles, not a shred of hesitation hidden in her heart as she moves the children behind her, trying to protect them.

Seeing the girl's decision, Ruth cackles.

"Then you shall die where you stand."

Suddenly, jagged roots grow up from the dirt, grabbing hold of the witch's victims, forcing them to the ground, trapped on their knees in terror, unable to move as the witch crawls closer and closer, until she is mere inches from them.

Yet she does not speak to the children. Why bother?

For one does not speak to the swine intended for the slaughter.

Instead, she speaks only to Red, biting anger at what the girl said.

"I led you to me. Did you know that? No one can find my cabin unless led there. Without me, you would have wandered the forest, this maze of trees, forever. Until one day you finally starved to death. But I… I heard your cries for help, and I took pity on you."

Ruth strikes Red's wound.

Red cries out in pain.

"You thought you could escape?" Ruth snarls. "This is my forest, child. I can feel its heartbeat, its pain. It belongs to me. With a single spell, I could burn it down…"

Lightning flashes. Thunder shakes the ground.

"Or cast a storm above it. Like the very storm you see above you now."

The witch pauses, grinning in satisfaction.

"I suppose the storm is no longer necessary."

In an instant, the storm stops.

"After all, it served its purpose."

No more lightning. No more rain. No more thunder.

Red's eyes widen at the sight, the vanishing of an entire storm, all the while Ruth merely grins, basking in their awed fear, as she reveals her true power.

Her true nature. A storm born for one reason.

"It brought you to me."

CHAPTER THIRTY-FOUR

The stranger's corpse lies in the dirt as the cabin slowly burns beside it.

Hollowed eyes stare up into nothing. Flesh sits open, torn apart and cut through. Blood stains his chest, having poured down from the wound that stopped his heart from beating, sinking deep into the soil below. Any

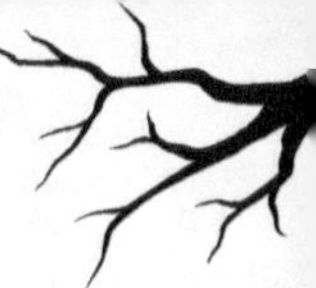

other night, the forest might have rejoiced at the taste of his blood. The ending of a curse.

The final salvation from the blight placed upon this land long ago.

But tonight, there are worse things than him in these woods.

So here at his death, the forest grieves.

After all this time, after all these years, his suffering is now over, his tormented soul allowed to rest. Just another victim of the witch. Just as the prince could not hear the burning cries of his beloved from within his buried grave, the stranger cannot hear the screams for help echoing from the girl in red, nor the cries of the children trapped, waiting for slaughter.

For the dead hear nothing.

Until something changes.

Even here, so far away, the witch's wicked devices can be seen as the storm clouds above vanish from sight, slowly revealing the night sky behind them, showing the light of a million stars, and the bright glow of the moon.

The *full* moon.

As moonlight bathes the forest below, slowly creeping across the ground, it touches the stranger's corpse. At first the light hesitates, finding its child dead, but that doesn't stop it. It keeps going, reaching out and pulling itself across his skin, digging into his flesh, enveloping the stranger's corpse in its haunting glow.

Until at last, something happens.

Something awakens.

The corpse's eyes regain their color, and breath fills his lungs once more, coughing up blood, as bones shift from within.

As the cruel agony of life takes hold, the stranger looks up to the night sky, seeing the full moon looming over the dark forest, and for the first time since his life was transformed into this living nightmare all those years ago, he welcomes its presence.

CHAPTER THIRTY-FIVE

As the helpless children cry and Red fights against the winding roots restraining her, Ruth stretches her arms out over the clearing within the trees and the bones lying scattered and disturbed in the dirt.

"This is where the legends started."

She walks slowly, feet treading against skulls as she does.

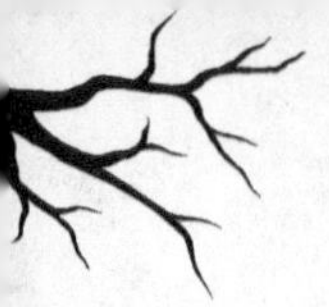

"The village hidden within the forest. The village that tried to burn me. Burn my sister. This is all that remains of them, every soul reduced to nothing more than a skeleton, rotting away in the dirt."

Moonlight shines across the forest as the branches twist the shadows, casting distorted darkness across the clearing, moving shadows that mimic the horrific tales as Ruth spoke them, first a fractured reflection of two young girls burning at the stake, then transforming with every spoken word.

"When we escaped with our lives, we swore we'd never return. But then I heard tell of the cursed forest, whose inhabitants had been slaughtered like swine, and I knew she had come home. To seek her vengeance."

Branches twist and shadows dance, revealing the slaughter Ruth spoke of: the original witch, murdering countless souls, never to escape.

"I came hoping she was alive, of course. Instead, I felt only the curse."

Ruth steps closer to Red, removing the hood from atop her head and brushing a wrinkled hand across her cheek.

"You see, child, the legends predate my arrival. I am the one who steals the children, that is true. But that is not the only horror within this forest."

Breathing deeply, taking in the night air, Ruth looks around at the field of bones.

"The animals who cry out in the night, only to be found the next morning, torn apart. The starvation that arises from it. The men who enter this forest, only to be found in pieces. The legends told of the evil, of the monster that lies within the trees. That is *her*. What my sister became."

Ruth holds her arms up at the majesty of the trees.

"The forest itself."

The witch's eyes cut back to Red, her prey, trapped helplessly.

"And now," Ruth laughs, "*I'll feed her your bones*."

Ruth's expression shifts to that of something barely human, eyes full of madness and unthinkable cruelty, and with the silver knife that appears in her hands, she is a second away from slashing Red's throat and spilling her blood as an offering to the forest when a voice stops her.

"Don't…"

The voice lingers in the air for a moment before Ruth turns to face the stranger, limping through the trees until at last he falls down to his knees within the clearing of bones, blood still dripping down from his chest.

Curiosity grows over the old witch's face.

"Forgive me," she says, "my memory isn't what it once was, but didn't I just kill you?"

Red's eyes find the stranger, thankful he's alive, not for her sake but for his. A friend not slain; a soul not sacrificed. But her heart softly breaks all anew when he looks back at her in solemn sorrow.

His eyes tell her the truth. He was better off dead.

Why, she does not understand. Not yet.

But truth comes soon enough.

"Tell me," Ruth continues, "what is to stop me from slashing this poor girl's throat before you even take a step?"

The stranger cuts his harsh gaze to her, and his fingers begin to twitch as he speaks the truth long since forgotten.

"Because I know what really happened to your *sister*."

Shock erupts in Red's eyes.

Ruth snarls in anger. "Do not speak her name."

"I didn't see it at first," the stranger continues, "but I do now. The family resemblance. The insanity. The arrogance of thinking the forest was yours."

Anger flashing in her actions, Ruth tightens her grip on the knife, turning from Red entirely and moving closer to the stranger, holding out the blade towards him as she growls with rage. "I will slaughter you where you stand if you speak another word of this heresy. Let's see if you get back up when I cut your heart out from your chest."

The stranger continues speaking, paying no mind to her pathetic attempts at a growl, nor her trivial threats, as his fingers keep twitching, more violently with each passing second.

"The witch, she did come back to this forest," he continues. "That much is true. But she did not come seeking revenge..."

He chokes on the words as he speaks them.

"She came to experiment."

Red's shock slowly fades, replaced with a growing nightmare as she notices even his eyes begin to flinch, as though something else was hiding behind them, waiting to crawl out of his skin.

"At first, she practiced on the animals," the stranger says as the trees once under Ruth's command seem to shrink away, terrified of something worse than even the witch. "Cursing them, deforming them until they weren't recognizable as living things. Trying to create something darker. Something unnatural. But then…"

Suddenly, his tone changes, as though the words were ripped from his very soul, as if still his heart cried out in distress from the memory of it.

"Then she made a mistake."

The stranger's head twists slightly, the bones in his neck seemingly snapping out of place. Even Ruth appears frightened as the stranger's words become growls.

"She cast a spell she did not understand, upon a child she did not know."

For a moment his eyes appear red, bright crimson blood filling them, drowning out all traces of a human iris, but he fights it back down as the rest of them stare in silent dread, knowing the truth before he even dares speak it.

"Your sister isn't the monster haunting this forest. I am."

Broken eyes cut to the skeletons littering the field.

"And these are not her victims. They are mine."

The stranger looks to Ruth, tone harsh.

"Her corpse lies among the rest."

The strong heart of Red stops in an instant as memories flash in her head. Of the monster that chased her through the forest. Of the beast that cut her leg. Of the claw marks left on the door after the stranger's arrival.

For another foolish moment, anger overtakes the witch's fear. "You're lying."

The stranger only looks to her. "You asked me how I knew it wasn't lamb…" Suddenly, his entire body distorts, and his eyes grow colder, voice becoming more a growl with each word. "It's because I've tasted it before. When the monster she put inside me ate her flesh, and sharpened its teeth on her *bones*."

For the first time, even Ruth steps back in sheer horror.

"The thing that witch put inside me. The creature that wants out. The legends call it a monster. But that night, when the moon first brought it out and it slaughtered everyone, they, the children who screamed…"

The stranger's eyes are overtaken with blood.

"They called it something else."

PART EIGHT:
THE
BIG BAD
WOLF

CHAPTER THIRTY-SIX

The stranger keels over, groaning in pain as more bones within him shift, and his voice becomes less and less human.

"It wasn't me, but I can still see their faces. Hear their screams echo in my mind. I can still see the blood, the torn flesh."

His body twists in agony as tears begin to fall from his blood-red eyes.

"I tried to kill it," he cries. "I swear I tried. To kill myself, rid this forest of the curse. But the wolf won't allow it. It won't die. It can't."

A vicious, inhuman growl escapes suddenly from his throat.

In terror, Red begins to fight against the roots that keep her trapped, trying to escape before the beast is unleashed upon them.

Ruth doesn't notice the girl breaking free from her snare, instead only staring at the stranger, attempting to hide the slight shudder in her hands.

"So, I stayed here," the stranger growls, "in this forest. I tried to starve it, keep it from hunting. But I still hear the screams, echoing in the night. I still wake up covered in blood. The blood of animals that wander into these woods, of men who come searching for their children."

More tears fall, making room for the blood that fills his eyes.

"But it's never enough. It's still hungry. That's why it chased the girl. That's why it followed the trail, why it led me to your cabin. It's still inside me."

The stranger screams in agony one final time before a moment of piercing silence grows as his eyes cut to Ruth, the witch who stole the children, growls erupting from his throat.

"And iT…Is… STARVING."

Bones crack beneath his face and his eyes lose any trace of humanity they ever had, glowing blood red as his body lurches forward in distorted pain, skeleton shifting, breaking flesh and tearing skin that's replaced with the pitch-black fur of an animal.

As the wolf begins to take over completely, what still remains of the stranger looks to Red, speaking a final word before his jaw breaks and massive fangs form from the splintered pieces.

"RUN!"

A tear falls slowly down Red's face as she watches in horror.

The stranger is no longer there. A monster now stands in his place.

The beast slowly stands up on two legs. Eyes of red, fur of monstrous black, teeth that could snap skulls like glass. It towers over them, massive claws hanging from its unnatural paws, as it growls softly into the night, staring right at its prey, the victim whose flesh it would rip apart. The witch whose bones would taste like the first meal it ever feasted upon.

Ruth.

At last, Red breaks free from the root's jagged grip before freeing the children. Yet even when released from their wooden bondage, still they stand paralyzed, looking up at the creature whom death itself fears.

Red herself takes one last look back at the monstrous wolf, shedding a final tear for the stranger she called a friend. Then, she takes the children's hands, and she runs. Runs out of the forest, away from the monster, vanishing within the trees and leaving behind the field of bones.

Ruth, however, backs up in terror, eyes wide as she looks at the creature her sister created, an unnatural beast unlike anything she's ever seen, and for the first time since the night they burned her, she is truly afraid.

The wolf snarls.

The witch runs.

The girl in red runs through the forest as fast as she can, trying desperately to escape with the lives of the children, even as she hears horrific growls echoing in the distance.

The witch is chased through her own forest, hunted down like nothing more than a deer running from a predator, and in her horrified haste she slips, falling down in the mud that she created with her storm.

The light of the moon casts a monstrous shadow over her as the wolf moves closer, red eyes glowing in the darkness, moving between trees as it grows ever nearer, growls of hunger coming with it.

Blood drips down Red's leg, escaping the bandaged wound as she runs, torn hood of crimson rising behind her in the wind.

The children run beside her in the dark, within the trees.

The raven follows overhead.

A low, unnatural growl echoes right behind her as Ruth stands from the dirt and runs once more, stumbling in terror to escape the beast, to make it back to her cabin. To safety.

Behind her, branches twist and break, trying to trap the beast that hunts her. Forced by spells to protect the witch. But as she looks back, she sees the wolf's shadow as it swings its massive claws, cutting a tree in two as though it were hollow, ripping past the branches as if they weren't even there.

Spells cannot stop what they have created.

"No," Ruth whispers in awed fear.

Streaks of crimson flash as Red runs through endless trees, a maze of wood and dirt that she doesn't understand, until

she becomes lost just as she had before. For the witch's words were true.

Nothing can escape this place.

She turns one way, then another, but no exit is in sight, no path to salvation.

Only more trees. Only the forest.

Finally, Ruth sees it. What so many others have seen before her. The light in the distance. The safety she is running towards. Like so many others, she believes the beautiful lie that it will save her from this grim tale.

Her cabin.

But something is wrong. The light appears too bright.

It is only after she reaches it that she sees the flames that engulf the cabin, and she falls to the ground, horrified tears of sorrow falling down her wrinkled face, as the promise of safety vanishes as it had for so many others.

For all the cabin offers is the setting for a feast.

Behind her, the red eyes grow closer.

There is no way out.

Red spins in agonizing fear.

There is no way out of this place. The witch's spells, the forest's own dark designs, it's a path that has no end,

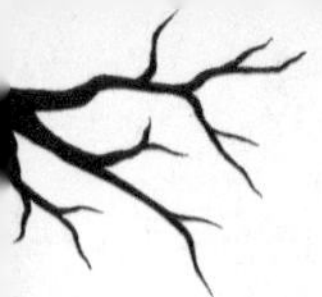

a prison of branches and leaves. Like the hidden spot beneath a child's bed, or a hood of scarlet, it's nothing but the sweet promise of an escape that will never come.

And so, the girl in red falls to the ground, crying as she does, tears of sorrow not for her own life but the lives of the children she promised to save.

The witch was right. They'll starve in this forest.

But then, Hansel points to something. A marking on a tree, a piece of wood carved from it. Then he takes a sharp rock from his pocket, revealing the source of the carvings, the promise he made to his sister.

"Trail."

Red looks in awe, tears vanishing as she sees it. The line of trees, all bearing the same markings. The trail the children created.

The way out of this forest.

Ruth cries in mourning as she looks to her home, burning as she herself once had.

"No," she sobs. "Not right."

Blood-red eyes escape the trees behind her as the monstrous beast moves closer.

"Not right," Ruth cries again, remembering the haunted words of her old friend. "Not right."

The wolf growls, and Ruth turns in terror to see it has followed her.

To see there is no escape.

Taking the children's hands, memories of torment no longer staying her feet, Red looks to the trail with resolve in her eyes and begins running.

The witch tries to move her hands, attempting to conjure up a spell, but the wolf strikes her, digging its massive claws into her flesh, turning her hands into a bloodied mess of torn skin and broken bones.

Screaming, she tries to run, knowing the beast would follow her into the back into the trees still living, so she tries to escape into those long dead, escape into her crafted cabin and the fierce fire.

Animals won't enter the fire.

The wolf strikes her leg, shattering her ankle as she reaches the steps, nearly taking her leg, but still Ruth crawls up onto her porch, pushing her way into the door, not yet aware it will be the last time she ever enters her precious cabin.

As Red and the children run through the trees, a raven calls out, following them to freedom from the sky above.

Ruth crawls inside the cabin's walls, passing over a line of burning fire as she does, wincing not from the pain of it but from memories of a pain far stronger. Finally, she drags herself to the middle of the cabin, where the fire has not yet reached, leaving a bloodied trail in her wake, as her visitor had only yesterday.

For a single moment, she breathes a sigh of relief.

Until the red eyes appear in the doorway, and she screams once more.

A flash of red appears between the winding trees as a raven swoops down to join them as they run, illuminated by the moonlight.

Ruth trembles as the wolf slowly walks into the cabin, through the fire.

"No…" she begs. "Please."

Fire spreads onto the wolf's dark fur, burning it as it moves closer, baring its teeth, red eyes wilder than the fire itself.

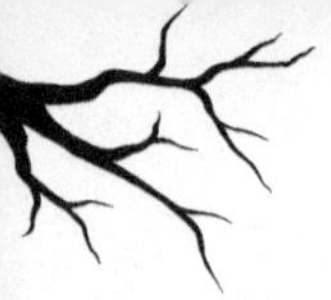

The witch backs away in desperation, but as she does, fire reaches her once again, and she winces, not wanting to be eaten, but not willing to be burned. In the corner of her eye she sees the princess, her corpse on fire once again, staring right at her as though she could see the witch's fear even from the grave.

As though the princess was laughing at the witch's slaughter.

Slowly, the wolf begins to growl once more as Ruth begs for her life. Then, as the cabin around them begins to crumble, walls collapsing from the fire's heat, the wolf strikes, slashing the witch's stomach.

Blood sprays from the wound, burning into ash before it even leaves the air.

The impact causes the flaming floor to collapse, and both monsters fall from the cabin into its basement, where the fire rages ever hotter.

As her body hits the ground, surrounded by skeletons of the children she'd murdered, the witch cries out in pain.

"Help me!"

Red runs through the forest.

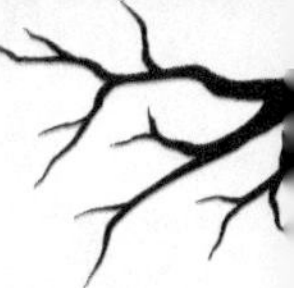

Ruth cries, body burning, blood spilling from her stomach, as she looks up at the wolf, the monster looming over her, pitch-black fur on fire, yet its eyes don't show pain.

They show hunger.

On and on they run, seeking to escape the nightmare before they become nothing more than victims spoken of in stories, in grim fairy tales meant to frighten children.

"No!" the witch cries out. "Please!"

The wolf growls and sinks its massive teeth into her shoulder, removing it from its place.

A trail of footprints line the mud as they approach safety.

The wolf strikes again, raking its claws across her chest, drawing blood that burns in the fire.

The witch tries to cry out, but the screams come out muffled as blood from her lungs catches in her throat, until, like the children she threatened, she cannot make a single sound.

A look of hope spreads across Red's face as she looks into the distance, seeing an opening within the trees.

Bloodied, half eaten, burning alive, Ruth stares up horror at the monster standing over her. A child of the moon, born of humans and bred of witches.

Her blood stains its teeth. Hunger fills its eyes.

Soon, it will starve no longer.

Surrounded by fire as her cabin crumbles, the witch tries to scream, and the wolf devours her.

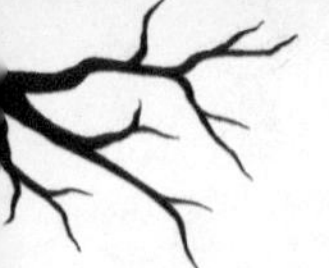

CHAPTER THIRTY-SEVEN

The girl in red escapes the forest.

Bursting through the final wall of trees, she falls to the ground, trying to catch her breath as thankful tears of unbearable emotion stream down her face. She tries to stop the crying, but she cannot. It's not fear, or sorrow, or even relief. It's just tears.

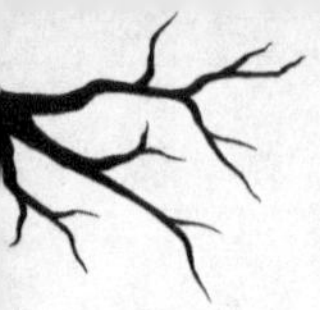

The aftermath of the horror she has escaped.

The forest she has survived.

Beside her, the children look back, still shaking in terror at the monster they witnessed. Red moves to them slowly, taking them in her arms, offering the comfort she had always longed for as she looks back into the forest, at its trees of rotting bark and twisting branches.

The moon glows above it.

A raven sits atop a branch, watching over them.

Now, as she looks into its once-haunting depths, the forest seems somehow brighter, as if it had escaped its torment the same as her. And in that moment, Red realizes why she cries. It was never the forest she escaped. In fact, the forest has done exactly what she hoped it would: save her from everything else.

All those years of being afraid. All those nights accepting the cruelty.

Thinking that no fairy tale could have a happy ending.

That she wasn't strong enough to deserve one.

She knows better now.

She is finally free.

Not from the scars, but from the pain.

And so, having no need for it anymore, she takes the crimson hood from her head, the place where she so often hid, and she wraps it around the children in her arms. Soon enough, it calms them as it always has her.

In the distance, she sees a light, rising above the trees, above the branches.

The fire they started. The flames that consume the cabin.

In the middle of a once-dark forest, a cabin burns.

On the night of her salvation, Red sheds a tear of loss once more, of sorrow for the friend she knew, the only one who ever saved her, who is now most likely gone along with the final traces of life within the forest.

In the basement of an evil cabin, a witch's skeleton lies covered in flames, next to the bones of her victims. Yet nothing else is there.

Nothing else consumed by the fire.

Red speaks a final word to the stranger who saved her.

Hoping that wherever he is, he hears it.

"Thank you."

Then, she stands up tall, strong, as she takes the hands of the children and leads them away. Back to their home.

Away from this twisted place. But as she starts to walk, something echoes, at first but a whisper, yet it stops her all the same.

Until, far away in the distance, echoing through the forest, Red hears it.

The thing that turns her gaze. The sound that brings a smile.

A sign of the monster that has survived.

The howl of a wolf.

HOWLLLLLL
THE END

MESSAGE FROM THE AUTHOR

Hey there, dear readers, this is Chad Nicholas.

First off, I just wanted to take this opportunity to say thank you so much for giving my story a chance. I know there are a million other stories you could read, and if you're anything like me you've got shelves full of books just waiting to be read, and so I'm truly honored that you decided to spend your time with these characters, and this story. The "locked-door murder mystery" genre has always been a favorite of mine, and if you've read my previous work, then you know how much I love werewolves and ravens, so getting to work on this story was truly incredible.

It means so much to me that readers like you chose to spend time in the stories that I write.

If you're here, you made it to the end, which hopefully means you enjoyed it.

I truly hope that you did.

If you did enjoy the story, please consider leaving a review. Reviews are so incredibly helpful when it comes to getting a book into the hands of readers, whether it be on Amazon, Goodreads, Barnes & Noble, or any other

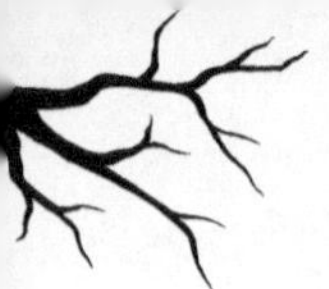

bookseller. Even a simple post on social media can make a world of difference for a novel's visibility. So, if you did enjoy it, please leave that review, make that post, and tell that friend!

And, hey, even if you didn't enjoy it, that's okay too. Whether the review is good or bad, it means you took the time to read it, and that's all that an author can truly ask for. So once again, thank you.

If you're interested in my previous work, I have released three other novels: a psychological horror titled *Nightmare*, a crime thriller titled *Shade*, and a slasher epic titled *The Animal*. You can find information on those in the following pages, along with a sample chapter from *The Animal!* If you liked the werewolf in this, I promise you'll love the Animal even more.

As for those of you who may be wondering what my next project will be?

All I can say is: brace yourselves.

The Copycat is coming…

ACKNOWLEDGMENTS

No author is an island, and that is never truer than in my case. As always, my deepest thanks must go out to my family for supporting me, both in my writing and in all other aspects of life. To my mother, my father, and both of my older brothers, I love each and every one of you.

Y'all are the reason I can write these stories.

While we say that books shouldn't be judged by their covers, I usually hope that mine are, because there are no finer cover artists than those at Miblart, whom I've had the pleasure of working with on four novels now. Not only are their covers incredible, but they go above and beyond with interior artwork, page designs, and formatting to make every book feel like a collector's edition. Without them, my novels would lose part of their voice.

Perhaps the most helpful to those of you reading this story is my incredible editor, Eliza Dee of Clio Editing. Without her contribution, the prose would lose part of its flow, the finer details of grammar would be forgotten, and even the simplest of words would risk being misspelled.

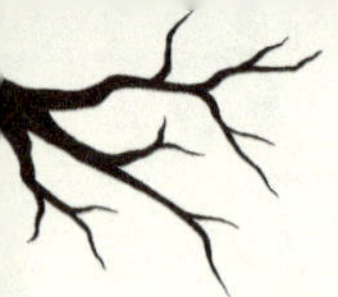

Once she's finished her copyedits and proofreads, I know the story is finally ready.

I would also be remiss if I didn't mention my college professor Michael Ward, whose theater class and final project were the inspiration for this novel. Thanks for the assignment, and the extra credit!

Also, a special shout-out to Saulo Zayas for his incredible book trailer, which inspired the font choice for the book cover itself!

Of course, *One Grimm Night* couldn't exist if not for the stories of the authors that came before me. I would like to sincerely thank Jacob and Wilhem Grimm for the fairy tales that they gave us. Without them, there could have been no Red, no Ruth, and no Big Bad Wolf.

And as always, I want to give my sincerest gratitude to all of the booktubers, reviewers, and bloggers who've reviewed my previous novels, *Nightmare*, *Shade*, and *The Animal*. Reviews are the lifeblood of marketing a book, but even beyond that, they truly do mean the world to authors.

Lastly, dear reader, thank you for reading this book.

I hope you read the next one too!

AUTHOR BIO

You probably never could've guessed this, but Chad Nicholas is an author. Shocking, I know. His skills as an author include writing words, occasionally editing them, and of course staring at his computer for hours on end, praying that the words write themselves. So far, that hasn't happened, and he's been forced to do it himself. To achieve this, he likes to rely on complicated plot twists, a healthy amount of crosscutting, and never-ending references to either crows, wolves, or both. Four novels in, there has yet to be one that didn't at least reference one of the two animals.

And rest assured, his next ones probably will too.

What can he say? He likes wolves and crows.

Ravens aren't too bad either.

In another surprising twist, this self-proclaimed author has actually written some novels before. Apparently "releasing books" is what all the authors are doing these days. His debut novel, *Nightmare*, was a psychological horror story. Next came a crime thriller titled *Shade*, and last but not least was his love letter to all things slasher, titled *The Animal*.

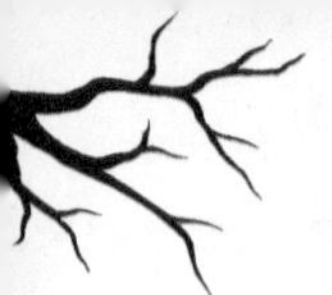

Chad is also grateful to have graduated with a master's degree in mechanical engineering from UT-Tyler. *Nightmare* was written the summer before his first semester, so he's humbled at how far he has come.

When he isn't writing, Chad enjoys watching movies, rewatching old superhero cartoons, reading comic books, and of course buying far too many action figures. On the gaming side of things, Chad's strangely proud to announce that he was ranked #1 in the world on the Teen Titan Challenge map from *Batman: Arkham Knight*, reached Onyx rank in *Halo Infinite Multiplayer*, and finally beat *Batman: Arkham Origins* on I Am The Knight mode, after only screaming with rage seventy-eight times.

If you're reading this, it means Chad has finished writing *One Grimm Night*—the twists just keep coming, don't they?—and is now working on something else.

This next story is going to be the best one yet.

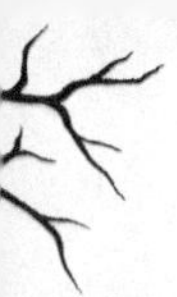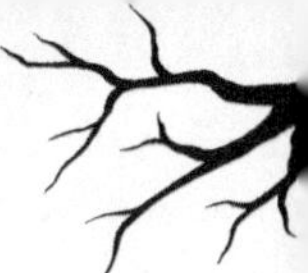

Keep in touch with Chad via the web:
Instagram: @thechadnicholas
YouTube: Chad Nicholas
Website: thechadnicholas.com

P.S. Once again, Chad has decided to request that DC Comics consider hiring him to write a graphic novel about Scarecrow's origin story. His obsession with Jonathan Crane only grows worse with each passing year, and I fear there is no helping him. At least, not until he can write the story that will prove to the world why Scarecrow is the greatest horror villain of all time.

Much more of this and we may have him committed. Writing the story would be much easier…

PRINCE'S JOURNAL

THE GIRL IN RED

REAL NAME:..

SUSPECTED OF:..

....

....

....

....

EVIDENCE:..

NOTES:

THE STRANGER

REAL NAME: ....

SUSPECTED OF: ....

....

....

....

....

EVIDENCE: ....

....

....

....

....

....

....

....

....

....

....

NOTES:

THE OLD WOMAN

REAL NAME: ....

SUSPECTED OF: ....

....

....

....

....

EVIDENCE: ....

....

....

....

....

....

....

....

....

....

....

....

NOTES:

THE OLD FOOL

REAL NAME: ....

SUSPECTED OF: ....

....

....

....

EVIDENCE: ....

....

....

....

....

....

....

....

....

....

....

NOTES:

THE WOMAN MISSING HER HAIR

REAL NAME: ....

SUSPECTED OF: ....

....

....

....

EVIDENCE: ....

....

....

....

....

....

....

....

....

....

NOTES:

THE BLIND PRINCE

REAL NAME: ....

SUSPECTED OF: ....

....

....

....

....

EVIDENCE: ....

....

....

....

....

....

....

....

....

....

....

NOTES:

THE CHILDREN

REAL NAME: ....

SUSPECTED OF: ....

....

....

....

EVIDENCE: ....

....

....

....

....

....

....

....

....

....

....

NOTES:

CONCEPT ART

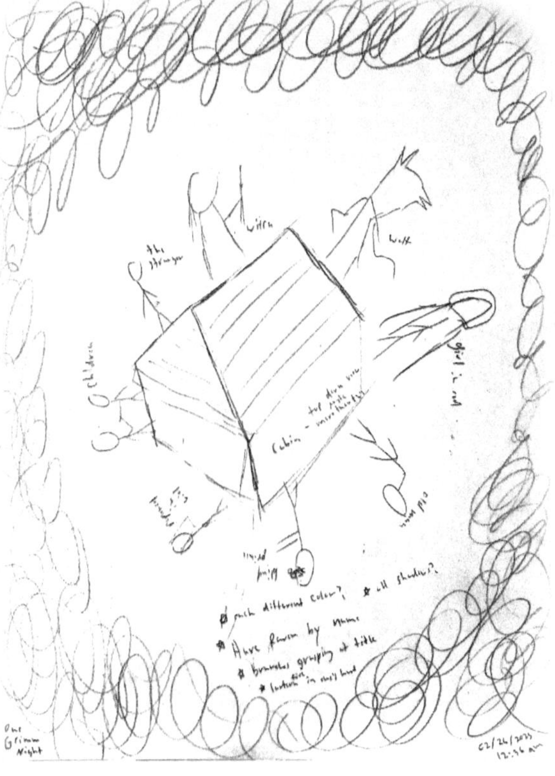

The initial rough sketch of the cover idea, drawn by Chad Nicholas. One night when he really should've been sleeping but was instead listening to music, the idea for this cover suddenly came into his head. Keeping the cabin front and center, it would feature the cabin's guests as shadows cast off it, with the haunted forest surrounding them all. Notice the basic quality of the sketch, a by-product of it being drawn at 12:56 a.m.

That same night, Chad drew another sketch, showcasing a variant layout that was kept simpler, with the cabin looming large in the center and Red approaching it. Here the quality is even worse than the previous sketch, as Chad had grown even more tired and only wanted to get the ideas down so he wouldn't forget them when he fell asleep.

Chad's second attempt at the cover, refining the layout and drawing more details. Here he kept the same base layout of the original concept, but rather than have Red be a shadow, he instead shifted her so that she was walking up to the cabin as in the variant sketch, creating a cover that was the best of both ideas.

As it was not drawn while he was half asleep, this sketch was much better.

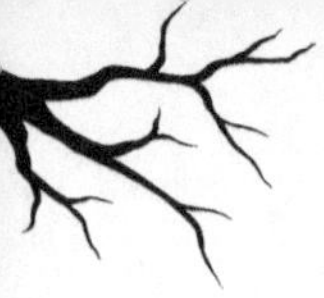

The final cover sketch done by Chad, adding more details, color, and the title.

From here, it would become the cover you see on this book.

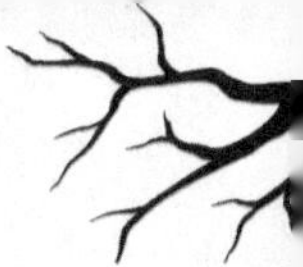

Chad's initial sketch for the back cover of the novel. Here he wanted a top-down view, with the tagline incorporated into the art. This was partially inspired by a fan made *Jaws* poster that utilized a top-down view of the beach with a shadow showcasing the shark. Here he incorporated his own designs for lowercase letters within the font and also staggered the size of the words to make each stand out.

Those trees took an eternity to draw.

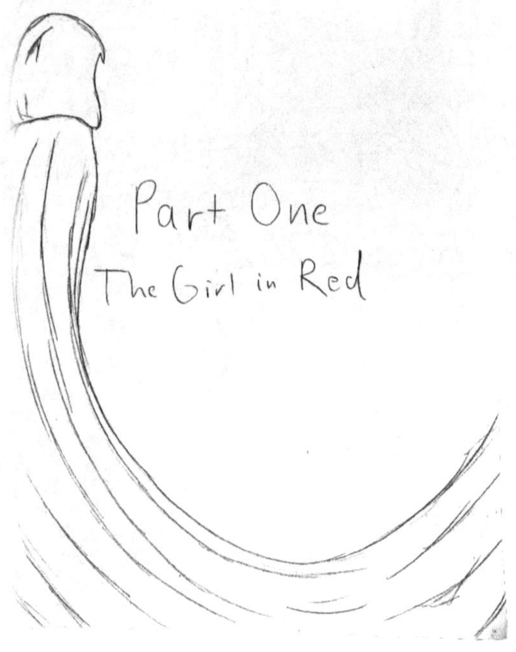

Rough sketch for Part One: The Girl in Red

For this design, since it was "Part One," the goal was to have it show Red approaching from the left and looking to the cabin on the right, whereas later on, the artwork for "The End" would show her on the right side of the page, looking back to the left. This was done to create "bookends" for the novel, with the two pieces of artwork mirroring each other.

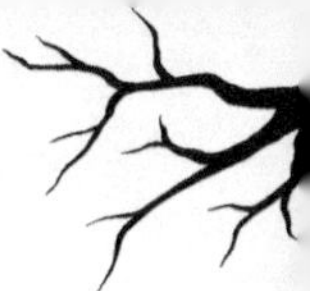

Rough Sketch for Part Two: The Stranger
One fun fact about this title page was that Chad used
sleeping dogs as a reference for how the Stranger was lying
in the dirt to subtly foreshadow his true nature.

Rough Sketch for Part Three: The Woman Missing Her Hair
Here the distinguishing factor for the sketch was the tilted head, which was intended to show the growing madness of Rapunzel. It was also during the drawing of this sketch that the idea arose to incorporate the characters' themes into the lettering, such as the letters in Rapunzel's name being on fire.

Rough Sketch for Part Four: The Blind Prince and
the Old Fool

The blind prince was sketched by Chad three separate
times for this heading, and that was the best attempt of
the group. Luckily, Miblart designs the final artwork.

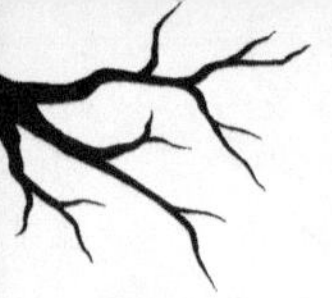

Rought Sketch for Part Five: The Dinner

Fun fact, the dinner scene was Chad's favorite scene to write.

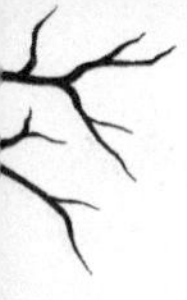

Part Six

The Children

Rough Sketch for Part Six: The Children
Thank goodness the lantern was tough enough to survive
the first fall, but fragile enough that the second time it
fell, it caught the entire cabin on fire.

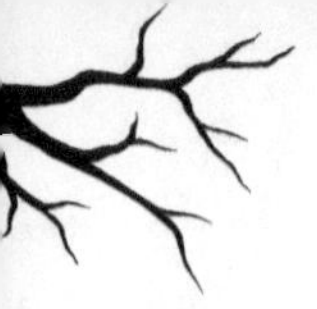

Rough Sketch for Part Seven: The Witch

Here the idea was to use the lantern to reveal Ruth's true nature, with most of the silhouette remaining smooth and gentle, whereas the closer it gets to the lantern, the sharper the lines become and the more burned her face appears.

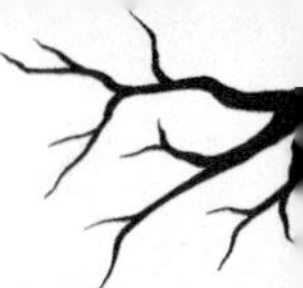

Rough Sketch for Part Eight: The Big Bad Wolf
Chad does love his werewolves.

Rough Sketch of the Chapter Heading Design
Originally the plan was to have the chapter headings alternate by POV character as in Chad's earlier novels, but the problem was that, because of the group dynamic, many chapters didn't have one dedicated POV character the way most stories would. So instead, the idea was to make one basic design that could be applied to every chapter, which is how the see-through cabin was born. This allowed for the artwork to mirror the story itself, with the goal being that the entire story could be told with the headings alone.
Though Chad maintains the writing itself was still necessary.

BY CHAD NICHOLAS
NIGHTMARE

BOOKS BY THE AUTHOR

NIGHTMARE

SYNOPSIS

Had it come back? No, it couldn't have. He had buried it for good. Or at least that's what Scott told himself. But what if it had? Was that why the scarecrow now watched him?

But the more Scott tries to ignore it, the more the evidence begins to pile up. So do the bodies. Because sometimes, the dead don't stay buried. Sometimes the monster survives.

As the bodies mount, and the secrets of his past grow more haunting, Scott must do whatever it takes to save his family. But what if by doing so, they find out what happened all those years ago? What if they realize what he did?

Scott learns that there is no escape from his own past, or the crows that have crawled out of it. He can only watch, as his life is turned into a living nightmare.

REVIEW QUOTES

"A Jekyll and Hyde for the modern age."

—John Mountain, Books of Blood

"This book was a page turner—the story was so interesting and fast paced that I almost read the whole book in one sitting. I thought I had it figured out so many times as far as where this story was going and I was wrong at almost every turn."

—Lezlie Smith, The Nerdy Narrative

"Nightmare is a psychological horror at its best!"

—Nichi, Dark Between Pages

"Chad might just be the plot twist master! Perfect pacing, great characters, extremely believable yet terrifying circumstances and amazing plot twists. This is now on my favorite Horror novels list for sure!"

—Ariel, Reading and Whatnot

"If this book doesn't give you a newfound fear for crows then I don't know what to tell you. This intense, twisting, murderous story kept me on the edge of my seat. After reading the first chapter my jaw had dropped and I found myself completely hooked! I had so many unanswered questions already and I felt nervous to carry on reading, not knowing what kind of twist and turning rollercoaster I was about to get myself into..."

—Claire Davis, Cup of Books

SHADE

ALL THEY HAD TO DO
WAS CATCH HIM

CHAD NICHOLAS

BOOKS BY THE AUTHOR

SHADE

SYNOPSIS

All they had to do was catch him.

At first, it was just another case, another serial killer to stop. They had done it countless times before; this time shouldn't have been any different. But soon, days turned into weeks. Desperation set in, and the victims started getting younger. What were they missing? Why couldn't they save the victims? They would have given their own lives just to stop that monster, to finally put an end to his killing spree. In the end, they almost succeeded.

But then, eight months ago, everything went wrong.

From the aftermath of one monster, a new one is born: a killer more lethal than they could have possibly imagined, like something ripped straight out of their worst nightmares. With it comes a new potential victim, struggling with the skeletons in her own closet, the guilt of past mistakes. And the longer she waits for the new monster to find her, to kill her, the more she questions if, deep down, she wants him to.

The desperate hunt for a serial killer, an ex-soldier losing his grip on reality, and a victim who's not sure she's worth saving come together as past and present intertwine in this explosive psychological thriller, which begs the question:

Can you stop a monster without becoming one?

REVIEW QUOTES

"A tale of twisting psychological horror that can be mentioned in the same breath as David Fincher's *Se7en*, and Michael Slade's debut novel, *Headhunter*."

—John Mountain, Books of Blood

"This crime story was filled with violence, gore, twists and turns that no matter how hard you look for, you'll never see coming. Chad Nicholas writes crack in book form, and I am so addicted."

—Lezlie Smith, The Nerdy Narrative

"This is a must-read for anyone that likes crime, suspense and action. The jump between the past and present keeps

the pacing on point and really adds to the suspense. My heart was pumping the whole time."

—Lana, Lore & Lullabies

"A phenomenal crime thriller. Just when I thought I had predicted things, I was instantly proven wrong. It was brutal at times, and deals with some horrific topics, such as grisly murders and severe PTSD, but it's handled brilliantly and vividly."

—Charles McGarry, Author of *The Nomad's Crucible*

CHAD NICHOLAS
THE ANIMAL

BOOKS BY THE AUTHOR

THE ANIMAL

SYNOPSIS

It came from the forest one night.

In the light of a full moon, it slaughtered seventeen people in their homes, leaving nothing but death in its path. Only one person saw its true face and survived, an eight-year-old girl named Riley found hiding underneath her bed, covered in blood, scared of a monster.

Now, twenty-five years later, it's happening again. A young girl is attacked in her home, forced to watch as her friends are slaughtered before her eyes by a monster wearing the mask of a wolf.

Or at least, she prayed it was a mask.

As the body count rises and the predator grows more violent, Riley is drawn back into the nightmare, forced to confront the horrifying monster she first witnessed all those years ago, surrounded by friends she cannot trust, and wolves she cannot see.

A scarred survivor, a group of hunted teenagers, and a sprawling forest full of wolves are brought together in this terrifying slasher, where only one thing is known for certain.

The Animal has returned, and everyone's a suspect.

REVIEW QUOTES

"Chad Nicholas has proven himself a master with his first two books, Nightmare and Shade, and he just raised the bar with this new slasher masterpiece. If you like slasher films, you will feel right at home with this one. With all the lights on and the doors locked of course."

—Charles McGarry, Author of
The Nomad's Crucible

"THE PLOT TWIST MASTER HAS BLESSED US ONCE AGAIN! A downright bloody, gory, traumatic homicide adventure. That is full of betrayal, secrecy, and the feeling that something is watching you. A SLASHER if ever read one!"

—Ariel, Reading and Whatnot

"If Michael Myers and Ghostface adopted and raised the baby from Stephen Graham Jones's *The Only Good Indians*, it would be *The Animal*!"

—Krystal Brooke, Goodreads Reviews

"You have to pick up this book. You will be sucked in and you won't want to put it down. I was camping when I read all 625 pages in 3 days! My heart raced and reading made me nervous. But I didn't want to stop!"

—Melissa Chung, Binge Reader

"The Animal literally caused insomnia for me, as I kept saying 'just one more chapter', even hours past my bedtime."

—Michele Eskelin, The Michele E YouTube Channel

READ THE FIRST CHAPTER NOW...

CHAD NICHOLAS

THE ANIMAL

CHAPTER ONE

The animal stalked its prey.

Hidden in the grass, out of sight and yet close enough to smell its prey's blood, the predator waited: muscles tensed, heart pounding, sharp jagged claws leaving trails in the broken dirt below as it opened its massive jaws and bared its bloodstained teeth. Drops of red fell from its mouth, remnants of its last meal staining the green field with a trail of death even as its ears twitched, and it began to search through the silence of the field, listening for the subtle, rhythmic sound of its prey's breathing, evidence

of a life soon to be taken. As it heard the innocent prey's gentle pant for air, the animal's eyes changed, losing what bit of life had appeared in them, replaced by mere darkness as its pupils dilated into black, lifeless holes, only focused on its next meal.

Mere breaths away, the prey stood, grazing peacefully, unaware of the horror that lurked within the shadows of the tall grass. Unaware of the predator seeking to rip it limb from limb and feast on the lifeless carcass that remained. But although no sound was made and no horrific sight revealed, instinct made the prey stop, a sixth sense revealing the truth as a mere feeling of dread, the sensation of a death soon to come, choking out all other senses and leaving only fear.

Something was wrong. A predator was nearby, and it had come for the prey's flesh.

As its legs trembled, the prey's eyes quickly scanned the grass, looking for any sign of danger, any sign of which way to run, even as monstrous images formed in its mind, fevered hallucinations of the creature whose teeth it could almost feel already sinking into its throat, draining the life from it.

What felt like an eternity of quiet dread passed, stuck in that frozen place between safety and slaughter, until finally the prey saw a pair of eyes hiding within the grass. Monstrous black eyes filled not with life but with hunger.

The lion pounced.

The gazelle tried to run.

In a single moment, every last nerve within the gazelle's small body erupted in a crazed, fear-induced panic, and it took off like a bullet. But it was far too late, for the lion's claws had already dug into its side, tearing through its shimmering brown fur and digging down to the exposed flesh below, cracking the ivory of its rib cage as the single strike brought the prey crashing into the dirt.

Still, the gazelle tried to fight. Frenzied, it kicked its legs in a sudden desperate attempt to find solid ground, anything to be able to run again. To escape. But when the lion's foot crashed down on its leg bone, breaking it in two, escape was no longer an option.

Screaming in mangled agony, tears of unimaginable pain streaming from its dying eyes, the gazelle began swinging its head, no longer thinking of survival, no longer thinking at all as instinct took over, the last remnants of conscious thought within a dying carcass, and it tried to push its razor-sharp horns into the lion's heart. The final hope of an animal too broken to run, too terrified to really fight, but still just alive enough to scream.

Its pain ended a moment later, when the lion's teeth ripped its throat in two.

"Yes!" Brandon screamed as he shot up off the couch, arms thrust upward in celebration as he watched the carnage unfolding on the television screen.

On the other side of the small sofa, Eric cursed as he slumped back into the cushions, defeated.

"The predator won," Brandon said, chest out and voice triumphant as he outstretched his open hand toward Eric. "Pay up."

Groaning, Eric pulled five dollars from his pocket and gave it to the victor of their little wager.

To their left, leaning back in a recliner, Kelly rolled her bright eyes in disgust. "What is wrong with you two?"

"Aww, let the boys have their fun," Britney said, leaning against Eric on the couch, grinning as he put his arm around her. "Besides, what's the point of a nature documentary if we don't get to watch animals kill each other?"

"Wow," Kelly said, acting too horrified to even look at them. "And my brother says I have issues."

"Where is your brother, by the way?" Brandon asked, equal parts mockery and actual question. "I mean, you said he was bringing us drinks and a movie, but we've been sitting here watching a nature documentary for the last hour. No offense, but I had higher hopes for this party."

"He'll be here," Kelly promised, despite being irritated with Rhett herself. What could possibly be taking him so long to show? She'd planned this party for four months. Not that it was hard to do when her parents were never around, but still, he was about to ruin it by showing up late on the worst night possible.

What could he be waiting for, a more dramatic entrance?

"You know Rhett loses track of time. He's probably on his way now."

"I hope so," Britney said, "because Eric looks way better when I'm wasted."

Eric grinned. "I have been told that before."

"Can we at least change the channel while we wait?" Kelly asked. "All the blood is grossing me out."

"Why don't we ask the new girl?" Brandon said, and soon their gaze focused on Megan, all of them turning to her in unison.

Kelly sighed to herself. Megan had been sitting next to Brandon all night, occasionally playing with her jet-black hair, clearly trying to get his attention. There was no way on earth she was going to back Kelly on this, even if the gazelle's death had made her visibly sick.

"I say we leave it," Megan said. "This is kinda interesting."

"Besides," Eric said, sitting up at attention, pointing at the screen, "it's about to get even better."

On the television, the lion had finished eating the gazelle and was now approaching a small lake, looking for a drink, something to wash the blood from its jagged teeth.

Unaware of the crocodile that lurked beneath the shallow waters…

"Round two! Predator meets predator!" Brandon howled. "Ten bucks on the lion."

"You're on," Eric responded, his last semilogical sentence before he began actually talking to the crocodile. "C'mon, Croc, you can do it. Avenge the gazelle!"

They waited in tense anticipation as the lion put its head down to the water and the crocodile moved closer. Any second now, one of them would move, and it would be a bloodbath.

The crocodile lunged.

The screen went black.

In an instant, darkness crawled over every inch of the house, enveloping the kids in a void darker than even the night sky, trapping them in its nothingness. Not a sound was made, not a heartbeat felt as suddenly they started shivering, imagining what could be watching them in the darkness.

What could have returned for more blood.

Anywhere else, it would have been brushed off: a simple power outage, nothing to fear. But in this town, on this day, the darkness could be felt in their bones, the memories of legends still spoken of. The thing that hid in the darkness of this town, waiting to hunt once more.

It happened so long ago…

A few minutes later, wax slowly creeped down from a dozen candles now scattered wildly across the room, illuminating the uneasy features of the five kids in a warm glow of flickering fire.

"Who's up for a ghost story?" Brandon asked, leaning forward so that his face hovered above the candles on the coffee table.

"I don't know if that's the best idea, considering," Kelly said, voice quiet. "You know what day it is."

"What day is it?" Megan asked, an innocent question from someone unaware of the nightmarish stories lurking within this town's history.

Kelly raised an eyebrow at the strange question. "It's the twenty-fifth anniversary."

"Of what?"

At first, not one of them dared answer her, as if whatever it was would rip them from their seats and drag them out into the darkness if they even dared speak its name. But finally, Kelly managed a hushed reply.

"The Animal."

Confusion creeped over Megan's face as she seemed to grow increasingly frustrated at their sudden secrecy. "What is the Animal?"

For a moment, each and every one of them looked at Megan in unsettled disbelief, as if not knowing about the Animal was the same as not knowing how to breathe. As if a piece of her was missing, a hollowness in her mind where the stories and the legends should have dwelled.

It was Brandon who finally broke the silence. "You don't know about the Animal?"

"No."

Still taken aback, Kelly found herself staring at Megan, wondering how it was possible. How could anyone in this town not have heard the stories, seen the houses still stained in blood, witnessed the forest where the beast had come from? The legend was a part of the town, a part of its people, a very real and monstrous myth that had changed everything.

To live in this town was to live in its shadow.

But then, Kelly finally remembered what should have been a simple explanation. Megan had only moved to this town a week ago. She was still an outsider, someone not yet marked by the legends. A single innocent soul amidst all the rest—probably the only one in the entire town who didn't know.

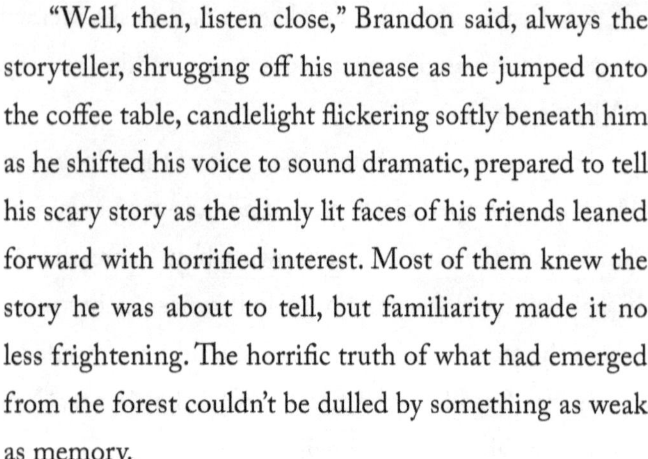

"Well, then, listen close," Brandon said, always the storyteller, shrugging off his unease as he jumped onto the coffee table, candlelight flickering softly beneath him as he shifted his voice to sound dramatic, prepared to tell his scary story as the dimly lit faces of his friends leaned forward with horrified interest. Most of them knew the story he was about to tell, but familiarity made it no less frightening. The horrific truth of what had emerged from the forest couldn't be dulled by something as weak as memory.

So there they sat, none more anxious than Megan, about to hear the legend for the first time, still naive enough to think that imagined monsters inspired more terror than those that truly existed. That nothing out there lurking in the darkness could ever be as terrifying as one's own imagination, when in truth, as she was about to discover with a trembling heart, it was the other way around.

Silence echoed for a second longer, frightened eyes glowing in the flickering fire, surrounded by nothing but shadows of a house, before Brandon began his story, fear creeping into even his voice.

"Twenty-five years ago, on this very night, the town was quiet. No sound could be heard in the streets, no bird could be found in the air. The light of a full moon cascaded down from the sky when an entire street of houses on the edge of the forest fell asleep, unaware of the horror that had escaped.

"That was, until the first family started screaming."

Tension filled the room as the words were spoken with such magnitude that even the candles' flames seemed to dim, as if attempting to retreat from the savagery once witnessed. As many times as Kelly had heard it, it still caused her heart to race, her breath to quicken in anticipation of something she knew wouldn't come and yet had feared all the same.

However, as she looked over at Megan, who was hearing the legend for the first time, Kelly felt a tinge of sympathy. The girl wasn't just nervous, she was terrified.

"What happened next?"

"The screaming stopped. For a few brief moments, the silence returned. Until the darkness moved into the next house, and the screaming began once more. On and on it went, an unspeakable horror moving from house to house, bringing with it screams of agony and death.

"When the police finally arrived, they found seventeen bodies, torn to shreds, most barely recognizable as human. In the end, though, the most terrifying thing wasn't the bodies left behind. It was what the police couldn't find. What had vanished without a trace. They searched the forest for weeks, trying to find any sign of what had killed the victims, any answer for what had caused the massacre. But they never did. The monster was gone."

Megan leaned in closer, jaw trembling as she spoke. "Did anyone survive?"

Brandon grinned. "Yes. A single victim. An eight-year-old girl who lived in the last house on the street. The police found her hiding under her bed, surrounded by her parents' blood and dismembered bodies, crying and twitching violently, repeating the same word over and over.

"Animal. Animal. Animal."

At that, Megan shuddered with fear, just as the rest of the town had ever since that night, hearing the only description ever given to the monster: the frightened words of a child who spoke a truth no one else would ever understand, for they hadn't seen what she had.

The Animal revealed.

"The legend goes that she didn't speak another word for months, her mind still lost in the horrors that she witnessed. Even when she did begin speaking, she never once spoke of what she saw in that house."

"What was it?" Megan asked, now visibly shaking.

"To this day," Brandon said, his voice growing solemn, "no one knows. Some say it was just a man, dressed in a costume, deranged and homicidal. Others, however, told stories about the monster that haunted the forest. The screams that could be heard there, even before that night.

A few old hunters will swear on their life that they saw a werewolf in the woods that night, massive, with black fur and blood dripping from its mouth. But in the end, the only real evidence for what killed all those people is the single terrified word of an eight-year-old girl. *Animal.*"

The anxiety-inducing dread that had once merely been felt now grew until it was all-consuming, as did the silence. For a moment they didn't even dare to blink, wishing more than anything that they had more than candles left to provide light. Because even growing up in this town, hearing the legend over and over again, could never really take away the horror of not knowing what had truly happened. Not knowing what could still be out there, in the forest, ready to devour.

More than the rest, Megan looked as though she might cry. "What happened to the girl?"

Brandon lowered his voice, once again trying to invoke fear. "The story goes that she still lives in that same house where it happened and never comes out. Some say she has gone insane, afraid of a monster that could be lurking outside. Others say she is the werewolf from the legend, and that she locked herself in a dungeon of her own making for fear of what she might do were she ever to be unleashed again."

"This story isn't true, right?" Megan said, no longer trying to hide her terror. "You guys are just messing with me?"

"It's true," Britney said. "Every word. You can still see bloodstains on the carpets of where it happened. The cleaners did what they could, but there was so much, and no one else has dared to live in the houses since. No one except the little girl."

Kelly piped in, feeling sorry for Megan but unable to resist at least mentioning it. "The forest that the Animal came from is the same one that rests behind this house. Legend has it the Animal is still in there, stalking its prey, waiting for its next meal."

"Let's go!" Eric said, suddenly excited as he leapt off the couch, pointing to the back door. "Let's see where it lives!"

"What?" Megan asked, terrified.

"C'mon," Britney said, following Eric to the door, brushing aside her unease. "It's the anniversary of the Animal. Live a little."

Both Brandon and Megan looked to Kelly, to see what she would say, to see if she would follow. Everyone always did that, looked to her to be the example, the leader.

Kelly shrugged. "Why not?"

They all stood on the edge of the porch, too afraid to step closer to what lay beyond the yard, merely fifty feet away.

The forest.

It was massive, stretching out for what seemed like forever, twisting through the entire town, corrupting everything with its endless expanse of dried dirt and dark trees. Looking at it now, at how the trees' dying branches choked out the moonlight, making the forest seem as though it wasn't even there, as if there was nothing alive behind the trees but instead merely shadows of things once living, Kelly couldn't imagine walking into it. Sure, she had gone in before, but not too far, and always during the day, never when it got dark.

Never at night.

Just like the rest of the town, a twenty-five-year-old story kept her from wandering through the trees for fear of the uncaught monster. The waiting beast.

The stalking animal.

"Okay, we've seen the forest," Megan said, quivering. "Can we go back inside now?"

"Don't you want to see inside it?" Britney asked, giggling. "See if the Animal is really out there." She turned to Eric, giving him a subtle grin and winking. "Go check it out."

Her smile made him blush, but he hesitated. "I don't know. I mean, looking at the forest is one thing, but actually going out there… I'm not sure."

"You don't have to go out there," Kelly said, trying to help give Eric a way out, even if she knew it wouldn't matter. Britney was her friend and all, but she had a bad habit of doing things like this. Pushing guys into doing stupid stuff, just to see if she could.

"Aww, come on, be brave," Britney said, once again giving him that smile of hers.

Eric looked into the woods, and as the darkness within it filled his eyes, he gave a slight shudder. "I don't know, Brit."

"What are you so scared of?" she asked. "The story of the Animal might be real, but that was twenty-five years ago. Whoever it was who killed those people is long gone by now. Besides," she said, adding the last bit to mess with his ego, "Dylan would go out there."

"Dylan's an idiot with no concept of danger," Kelly said. "He would jump in a shark tank covered in chum just for a laugh."

"Or," Britney continued, turning Kelly's point into her own, "he would go into the woods to impress the pretty girl. It's not even a full moon."

Kelly rolled her eyes, but she also knew at this point it wouldn't matter. Nothing could stop it now as Eric took a deep breath and, given no choice, he started toward the woods, his path faintly lit by thin traces of moonlight that escaped from the clouds above.

Step by step he grew closer to the vast expanse of darkness that seemingly lay behind the trees, the darkness that had once held a monster, and as he grew ever closer, his hands trembled.

"You don't have to go out there," Kelly said, loud enough for him to hear across the yard.

The rest of them watched in complete silence, waiting for something to happen. For some creature to reveal itself at any moment and charge at Eric with twisted teeth and broken claws, wailing and snarling as it left the deceased shadows of the forest and attacked those still breathing.

But nothing came.

At least not yet…

Fighting the urge to run, Eric took another step, and his outstretched hand pressed against the rough bark of a hollow tree, long dead, its rotting corpse held up by twisting roots, unwilling to let it fall, to let it rest, instead keeping its carcass standing as a reminder of the death that lay within. As Eric's palm scraped against the bark, he felt the fear it instilled flow across his skin and bury itself within his bones. He was on the edge of the forest now, only a single step from entering its depths and facing whatever lay within.

Suddenly, Kelly saw something move in the forest.

Eric took one last breath and stepped in, closing his eyes as he did.

"Eric, come back," Kelly said cautiously as she searched the forest for the movement that caught her eyes.

As Eric's foot hit the ground, the gravity of the forest faded for a moment, and relief washed over him as he turned around to see his friends watching him from across the yard. Standing within the forest, he held his hands up in victory, the last happy moment he would ever experience, before he heard something: a faint noise coming from the woods, coming from behind him. It almost sounded like...

Growling.

"Get away from that tree!" Kelly screamed as her eyes saw the horror.

Growling echoed throughout the forest as the thing hidden within the trees leapt at Eric, bringing him to the ground in an instant, and before his body could even gasp for air, Britney was forced to watch in shocked terror as the unnatural thing still shrouded in darkness, looming over Eric, began to claw at him. Soon it drew blood from his chest, the shimmering splatters of red contrasting the darkness of the creature, signaling the death it had brought. As the forest grew painted with crimson, the new victim wailed in torment, unable to leave the forest he had entered, forced to die within its cold grasp.

Eric's screams of agony were soon silenced when his body went limp.

It was only then, after its prey was slaughtered, that the creature finally stood up, slowly turning its gaze to them as though it hungered for more blood. Covered by the forest's shroud of darkness, it stepped closer. It walked almost like a man, though hunched down, but its body was distorted and covered in something inhuman. Something grey.

Britney's body froze in terror.

What is that thing?

"Run!" was all she heard as Kelly grabbed her arm and pulled her backwards toward the house, like a desperate shepherd trying to drag its lamb to safety, knowing that safety wouldn't come, for the wolf had already tasted blood.

Yet still, they ran.

The creature followed.

"It's coming," Britney screamed as she saw it run, wild and frenzied, its horrific growling only echoing louder as it grew closer. Her mind began to panic. How could it be real? How could something like that exist? Something so… inhuman.

"Get in!" Kelly screamed as she pulled Britney through the door and shut it behind them mere moments before the creature crashed into it. But while the door might have kept the monster at bay, its bloodthirsty growl still echoed through the cracks, filling the house with the sound of its hunger.

It wanted in. It wanted *them*.

"The car!" Kelly cried as they moved through the house toward the front door. "We have to go now!"

As they ran, however, fear took hold of Britney once more, and she collapsed on the floor, too paralyzed to move, even as her mind begged for an escape, forcing her into a wretched state of distress and terror.

Knowing they couldn't stop, Kelly motioned for Megan to help Britney up as Brandon made it to the front door.

"Ready?" Kelly asked, now beside him, both staring at the wooden door in fear, imagining the creature that lay beyond it, still stained in Eric's blood.

"You stay here," Brandon said, voice shaking. "I'll go first, in case it's still out there. Then I'll back the car up for all of you."

Kelly looked to him, clearly stricken with fear, but still trying to be brave, to do the right thing. She respected him for that. "Are you sure?"

"No," he admitted, choking back a nervous gulp as he ran out the door into the cold night air where no walls could protect him, moving desperately toward the lone car revealed in moonlight.

For a few brief seconds, it looked as though he would make it. Even Britney stopped crying as she watched him run, giving them all a fleeting hope of survival, until he was less than five feet from the safety of the car, and the creature with grey fur revealed itself on the other side, rising from the darkness like a wraith, a symbol of death itself, before leaping over the hood and tackling Brandon to the ground, growling viciously as it cut into his chest. The boy's screams were silenced in mere seconds, but the creature didn't relent, lashing out in a frenzy of grim, bloodied slashes.

As though it was losing control.

The night was dark. Clouds covered the sky like a black veil, blocking out any trace of light from the stars. But as the monster stood hunched over the boy's corpse, the moonlight that escaped the clouds was just bright enough to make out one single aspect of the creature's face.

It wasn't human.

Britney began screaming.

The creature turned its head toward the sound.

Kelly slammed the door as fast as she could, not waiting to see what it did, not waiting to see if it would attack the sound or continue to mutilate its already disfigured prey.

"We're gonna die," Britney cried, and Megan began weeping as she paced the floor, wishing she was already dead.

"No, we're not," Kelly said as she ran frantically around the room, checking the locks of every door and window, before finally sitting on the floor beside Britney, taking her head in her hands, and looking into her eyes.

"Listen, we are going to be okay, but we have to stay calm. We can't call the cops because we don't get reception this close to the forest, and we can't go back outside. So, we have to stay in here and hope that it can't get in."

For a moment, it looked as though she might get through to Britney. But then something crashed into the upstairs floor, echoing throughout the entire house, a sign of what had already entered.

Britney tried to scream, but Kelly covered her mouth. That didn't stop Megan, though, who screamed so loud that the police might have heard it from across town. A scream that caused birds from the forest to scatter into the night.

But far more haunting than the scream were the footsteps echoing from upstairs, each one in quick succession. Whatever was above them, it was running.

"How'd it get in so fast?" Britney asked, terrified.

"I don't know," Kelly said, trying to think. "There's a knife in the kitchen," she said, dragging Britney and motioning for Megan to follow. As they ran, the creature could be heard descending the stairs.

They didn't have much time.

In the center of the kitchen was an island, just tall enough that it shrouded the other side in darkness, even when there was light. Resting atop it was a single knife. There were more in the drawer, but the footsteps from the stairs stopped, and they were out of time. Kelly went for the knife, but as she grabbed it, she caught a brief glimpse of something inhuman moving through the darkness by the kitchen doorway, and she dropped to the floor, bringing Britney and Megan with her. They hid, crouched down behind the island, hoping the creature wouldn't find them.

The image she'd glimpsed burned in her memory.

The creature, it wasn't just inhuman.

It wasn't natural.

Footsteps grew closer.

Britney didn't allow herself to breathe, thinking if she did it would hear her. It would kill her. She didn't want to die. Not like this.

She heard growling. It was coming from behind the island, a monster hidden in the shadows of the house, and it was moving toward them. Her heart started to race. The creature had found her. *No!*

The creature leapt onto the island, and through the darkness, Britney saw an outline. Legs bent, poised to pounce, arms reaching down to the island's granite top, body bent over them, moving unnaturally, almost agile. Face-to-face with the three of them now, it tilted its animalistic head, and for a single moment, it didn't move at all: a predator waiting to pounce, staring at prey who were waiting to be slaughtered.

It lunged at Kelly first, striking her in the head and stabbing something into her stomach. She squealed in sudden pain before moving to bring the knife down in its neck, but it

caught her arm and struck her again, knocking her back into the cabinets behind her, the impact cracking them. Then, her body simply fell to the floor below, head bruised, sight fading.

Dizzied, Kelly lay there in agony, clutching her bleeding stomach, as the creature turned its attention to the other girls.

Megan screamed as it stabbed something that looked like a bone into Britney's stomach, and then her throat, killing her in an instant. But death didn't stop the creature's torment, and it kept stabbing her, over and over, until blood covered every inch of her once living skin.

Frozen in horror, Megan looked at the monster, still partially cloaked in the shadows of the house. Grey fur, a beast's head, feral movement. But the way it stabbed her. The cruelty of it. That part seemed almost human.

"Run!" Kelly screamed as she pulled Megan away from the monster, still clutching her side, and grunting in pain as blood streamed from the wound. "She's already dead. We have to run."

Finally, a resolve grew in Megan's eyes, and they took off through the house, Kelly frantically grabbing a flashlight from a drawer as they did. Before they could even think, they were out the door, through the driveway, and onto the road, running so fast they couldn't feel their legs, desperate to get away, adrenaline kicking in as they tried to fulfill their most basic instinct.

Survive.

They had to have run almost a mile, feet dragging against a gravel road, surrounded by the forest on either side, when Megan's body finally gave out and she slowed down, lungs bursting, barely managing to stay upright as she looked behind her, expecting to see safety, nothing but an empty road and a hollow forest.

But the beast was chasing them, less than thirty feet away.

How had it gotten to them so fast?

It ran on two legs, arms flailing wildly as it growled. The sound sent a sudden shiver down Megan's spine as she cried, pleading with anyone who would listen to save her.

A blood-curdling shriek echoed through the air.

Kelly turned in terror to see something on top of Megan, slamming her head into the ground, attempting to crush her skull. Instinctively, Kelly shined her flashlight at it, and for the first time on that dark, horrific night, she saw the beast clearly. It was massive, covered in grey fur that held distorted eyes, a long nose with sharp teeth, and an expressionless face now drenched in blood. As the light

hit it, it looked to the moon and howled, standing over its fallen prey.

Then its eyes turned back to Kelly.

In a flash of movement, she ran down the country road as fast as she could, clutching her bleeding side, waving her flashlight in the air. In desperation she searched for anything, anyone at all, all the while wondering how far away the monster was.

Wondering when she would hear it growl.

Then she saw it. Headlights.

She dropped to her knees in the middle of the road, holding up the flashlight, blood streaming down her stomach as well as her head, screaming at the top of her lungs.

"Help me!"

The car stopped beside her, and an elderly man stepped out in shock, seeing the blood as she began to cry. As he approached her, the two of them alone in the light and surrounded by darkness, he asked her a single question. "What did this to you?"

Her voice quivered as tears streamed down her face.

"*Animal.*"

www.ingramcontent.com/pod-product-compliance
Lightning Source LLC
Chambersburg PA
CBHW051439190726
48289CB00001B/255